THE FRANKLINS

NICOLE NEWMAN

NICOLE NEWMAN BOOKS

Copyright © 2025 by Nicole Newman – All rights reserved.

Published in the United States by Nicole Newman Books, an imprint of O-Live! Theatre LLC, Phoenix, Arizona

Nicole Newman Books is a registered trademark of O-Live! Theatre LLC.

Library of Congress Control Number: 2025911502

Paperback ISBN – 979-8-9991147-1-6
Hardback ISBN – 979-8-9991147-0-9
Ebook ISBN – 979-8-9991147-2-3
Audiobook ISBN – 979-8-9991147-3-0

Printed in the United States of America on acid-free paper

CONTENTS

FROM THE STAGE TO THE PAGE

Another Cinderella Story

Esther's Journey

Holiday Gatherings (The Franklins)

Katrina's House

Sister Mary's House

Summer Raine

A Summer Raine Christmas

This novel is inspired by the stage play
Holiday Gatherings — a production that captured hearts
in theaters and now invites you into the deeper, written
world of The Franklins.

*Nicole Newman is a playwright expanding her creative
reach by turning her stage plays into books. She believes this
allows her to explore stories in a new and exciting way —
and to connect with readers in a more intimate way.*

www.nicolenewmanbooks.com

From stage plays to books,
I dedicate my deepest love to my children
Ariana, Nicholas, and Noelle,
to my Mom and Dad, my brothers GreGory and Isaac,
and all the people I hold dear.
-Nicole

THE FRANKLINS

CHAPTER ONE

LILA & HENRY

THE DREAM BEFORE CHRISTMAS

In Lila's dream, Selena's voice trembled as she screamed her daughter's name, the sound drowned out in a whirlwind of camera flashes and the dazzle of glittering gowns. Blinded by pulsing spotlights, she stumbled forward, weaving frantically between the sleek black SUVs lining the edge of the red carpet.

Her heart hammered as she frantically scanned every tinted window, straining to hear the faintest cry of her child. The roar of spectators and the relentless throb of music closed in on her, suffocating. But Selena pushed forward—desperate to find her little girl before it was too late.

Only a few steps away, her brother Sam squared off against her husband, their voices rising above the glamorous hum of onlookers. Sam's voice cracked with outrage as he practically spat the words:

"You're not taking that child—do you hear me?"

Her husband's reply vanished into the buzz of murmuring guests, but the icy glare in his eyes—dead cold—told Selena everything she needed to know: he had no intention of backing down.

Suddenly, Lisa and Bo burst through the crowd, their faces tight with alarm. "What's going on?" Bo demanded, eyes darting between the line of cars and Sam before locking onto Selena's wild, desperate gaze.

Before she could respond, a noise pierced through the chaos—sharp, suddenly closer. Panic, like a sudden frost, spread through her veins. Selena spun toward the sound, only to be engulfed by another dizzying surge of light and loud noise from the crowd. She glimpsed her siblings lunging forward, their faces twisted in fear, before darkness swallowed everything.

Lila gasped sharply, bolting upright as her hand flew instinctively to her chest. Her heart slammed against her ribs, each beat echoing the ghostly sound of Selena's terrified scream. She squeezed her eyes shut, fighting desperately to silence the lingering cries still ringing in her ears.

Slowly, the familiar shapes of her bedroom sharpened into focus, shadows swaying gently in the moonlight. The comforting scent of pine from the Christmas tree mixed reassuringly with the crisp fragrance of freshly laundered sheets, pulling her fully into the present.

Only then did she register the softness of the bed beneath her, the peaceful rhythm of Henry's breathing beside her—safe, steady, and undisturbed. Yet fragments of the dream still clung to her, twisting like shadows at the edge of her thoughts, whispering warnings she wasn't ready to unravel.

Was it simply a nightmare, or had something deeper stirred beneath the surface of sleep?

"A dream," Lila whispered, her voice trembling slightly as tension drained slowly from her shoulders. *"It was just a dream."*

Pulling back the sheets, Lila glanced to her left, where the alarm clock next to her jewelry box on the nightstand glowed with blue numbers reading 4:00 AM.

Barefoot on the plush carpet, she moved with quiet resolve—each step a silent prayer, an appeal for guidance in a night filled with uneasy visions. She quietly crossed the room towards the small antique writing desk nestled in the corner by the window.

Lord, what are You trying to show me? she silently prayed.

The smooth, cool surface of the desk met her fingertips as she reached down and pressed the switch with a gentle click. The soft glow of Christmas lights instantly painted the outline of the window panes in a warm, festive hue.

A worn, leather-bound notebook lay open, its creamy pages slightly yellowed with age. This notebook was her confessional, a place where dreams and fears danced together in ink.

Lila's hand trembled as she recorded the details. Why would Selena's husband barge onto the red carpet of an award ceremony? Threatening to take a child. A child who, in real life, is already a teenager? she wondered.

What disturbed her most was Sam's rage—she had never seen her eldest son so livid, as if he were on the verge of throwing a punch.

And where were Bo and Lisa? They'd appeared in the crowd, but somehow remained oblivious to the confrontation.

The inconsistencies left her uneasy; the child in the dream had seemed so young, so vulnerable—far from the teenager her granddaughter really was. Lila's scribbled notes reflected her growing worry that each distorted piece, each inexplicable burst of anger or missing voice, carried a deeper meaning.

Was this God's way of showing me something beneath the surface? she wondered, pressing the pen harder onto the page. The dream felt like a warning—one she couldn't afford to ignore.

Her grip trembled as she signed and dated her journal entry, the pen a firm anchor in her hand. As she rubbed her hand, a deeper worry settled in: What secrets might her children be keeping??

Am I praying enough for them? Am I listening?

Looking over at her sleeping husband, Henry, Lila offered a silent prayer as she gazed out the window. The grandfather clock in the living room, though muffled by distance, startled her from her thoughts.

The first rays of dawn were just beginning to peek through the window. It was 5:00 AM. She closed her eyes as the familiar sound of five deep notes resonated through the quiet house, letting the vibrations ground her.

Slowly, Lila opened her eyes, and watched as the morning light crept into the room. Her fingers traced the familiar groove of a deep scratch in the antique desk, the rising sun illuminating its jagged edges.

A sigh escaped her lips as she remembered her mother's words about the cherished heirloom.

"A scar is a reminder of where you've been, but it doesn't have to dictate where you are going."

If only my mother were here to help me decode this dream, Lila thought. Crossing her arms to her shoulders in a hug, self-soothing as she sat in quiet reflection.

"What is it, my dear?"

Henry's voice broke through her reverie. With a shuffle of the bedsheets, he pulled back the comforter and reached for his housecoat. He walked to her side, and placed his warm hands on her shoulders.

Needing his reassuring presence at that moment, Lila turned to her husband, her eyes glistening with unshed tears.

"Every time I have a dream this vivid, Henry," she confided, her eyes searching his sleep-softened face, "it usually means something."

She recounted the details, her voice hushed as she described each scene. Henry listened intently, his brow furrowed with concern. When she finished, he held her close, the warmth of his embrace soothing her troubled heart.

"Dreams can often be prophetic warnings," Henry said, his voice gentle yet firm.

"Well, for now let's just be mindful to beef up our prayers. We can't let fear overshadow the joy of Christmas. We have a party to get ready for today."

Lila nodded, she shouldn't start the day off with worry. After all, she had written the dream down and it would be a reminder on how she should pray.

"From your mouth to God's ears."

She whispered, clinging to the hope inherent in the old phrase. Henry squeezed her hand, understanding her unspoken fears. He rose, his movements gentle as he reached down and kissed her forehead.

"Amen," he murmured. "Let's go have our coffee. We have a big day ahead of us."

Lila took a deep breath and nodded as Henry headed down the hallway to the kitchen. Grateful for the comforting respite of their morning routine.

Closing her journal, she walked over to the closet to quickly change into the snowman moo-moo she had laid out the night before. Feeling the soft flannel warm against her skin, she inhaled as the aroma of coffee filled her senses.

Drawn by the strong scent of dark roast, she hurried down the hall to find Henry had already poured her a cup in her favorite Christmas mug.

As she took her usual seat at the breakfast nook, the steam from her coffee swirled around her face, the warmth of the mug in her hands offering a small measure of comfort. Her gaze drifting to the framed photos of their family adorning the walls.

Sam, her eldest. His serious expression in the photo was so like Henry. But lately, their phone calls had left her with a prickle of unease.

Like his father, he'd always been one to share the details of his work, a natural storyteller. Now, his answers were clipped, the conversation brief. A hidden worry? She couldn't name it, but the change in him was undeniable.

As Lila blew the steam on her coffee, a familiar warmth spread through her chest. Yet, a persistent feeling tugged at her as she stared at Selena's picture beside Sam's. Beaming, her smile wide and carefree.

But as she sat there, a nagging feeling returned—Selena hadn't been entirely open with her lately. Their last conversation had felt... reserved. Almost like she was holding something back. Distant.

Stirring a spoonful of sugar into her coffee, her gaze drifted to the photos of Bo and Lisa, their arms slung around each other, laughter etched on their faces.

They were always the lighthearted ones, quick with a joke, eager to reassure her that everything was fine. But sometimes, their reassurances felt a little too quick, their carefree attitude almost a performance. A tiny seed of doubt always lingered.

Am I doing enough? she wondered.

"A penny for your thoughts, Mrs. Franklin?"

Henry teased gently, pulling her back to the present.

Lila reached out, her hand finding his across the table. She loved the way her husband of 56 years didn't push too hard when he knew she was worried. They often sat in silence as he let her comb through her thoughts without prying to much.

"Just thinking about our children, my love, and praying that today's Christmas-Eve party is peaceful and has no major conflicts." Lila's gaze drifted to window as she spoke, a worried smile gracing her lips.

"I hope they'll all be on time today. You know how we're always waiting on someone to get here before we can all sit down and eat." Henry chuckled, the warmth in his eyes softening the lines around his mouth.

"Indeed. They certainly didn't inherit our punctuality."

Lila continued, her smile fading as a shadow crossed her face. "And I pray the girls will be civil to each other. Last year's tamale debacle was quite the spectacle."

A shudder ran through her as she recalled the heated argument between Selena and Lisa, their voices sharp as knives as they bickered over who deserved the last batch of tamales to take home.

It was such a spectacle, the whole house cleared and everyone ended up outside while the girls argued to the top of their lungs. It had been a tense and uncomfortable ending to an otherwise joyful gathering.

"This year will be different," Henry promised, reaching across the table to squeeze her hand.

"Let's make sure they get equal amounts of tamales to take home." Henry joked as they chuckled remembering the scene.

Lila nodded, a lingering doubt remained. The strained relationship between her daughter's was something she'd been praying about for years, she often even wondered if she'd done something wrong raising them. Selena and Lisa were like water and oil.

Under her breath, she said a silent prayer for peace and harmony as she took another sip of her dark roast coffee, savoring the caramel notes of her creamer. The rest of the morning was spent in a flurry of preparations.

Lila found comfort in the familiar haven of her kitchen, softly humming Christmas carols as the melody danced between the cheerful clatter of pots and wooden spoons. The rich, smoky aroma of refried beans simmering with a ham hock rose in steamy waves, curling around her face. With each slow stir, she poured the worry left behind by the night's dream into something steady—into love, into care, into the food she was preparing.

Beside her, a pan sizzled and sputtered, releasing the savory scent of butter as she browned the Spanish rice to a golden hue. The caldo, a fragrant broth bubbling gently in a nearby pot, promised to add warmth to the dish.

Onions and peppers, a vibrant mosaic against the worn wooden chopping block, fell to the rhythmic thud of her knife. Each movement executed with precision, and infused with heartfelt passion.

Meanwhile, outside on the patio, the air crackled with the inviting sizzle of marinated ribs and chicken as Henry's weathered hands expertly tended to the grill. Plumes of fragrant smoke, carrying the tantalizing scent of charred meat and sweet barbecue sauce, drifted across the yard.

The Franklin family home had always been the heart of their holiday gatherings—a place where laughter echoed off the walls and the feast was always met with cheers of "best ever!" It was the kind of joy Lila and Henry lived for.

As Lila set the timer for her cakes, her gaze drifted to a worn scuff on the floorboard, its faint outline catching the light. She closed her eyes, lifted her chin, and breathed a quiet prayer.

Please, Lord, help us find peace even amidst the chaos, her eyes returned to the scuff. *"Let this Christmas be drama-free."*

CHAPTER TWO

SELENA & JORDAN

UNVEILING SHADOWS

The sting of his slap sent a shockwave through her body. Her cheek burned with a fiery heat as the taste of copper filled her mouth. Her bare feet froze on the cool marble floor as she ran into the bathroom.

How could this happen now? Selena wondered, her heart pounding with a mix of fear and disbelief. Of all the times, why this moment?

Selena's reflection stared back at her from the mirror, her eye throbbing, the skin already beginning to swell. The air crackled with her husband's rage, and the deafening high-pitched ringing in her ear momentarily threw her equilibrium off.

Why had he chosen this time, she wondered, knowing that the family Christmas party was just a few hours away?

A bitter sense of irony laced her thoughts as she winced, her fingers delicately brushing her skin. Here she was, meticulously applying makeup—a symbol of beauty and self-care—to hide the physical evidence of her husband's violence.

She dabbed a layer of concealer on her bruised skin, a layer of foundation, a touch of powder—each stroke a desperate attempt to mask the pain he had inflicted.

Every swipe of makeup felt like burying a memory, a secret too painful to show. *But what else can I do?* she thought, as she fought back tears.

The tumultuous chain of events had been set in motion by a heated argument with her husband, Richard—one that revolved around how much money Selena had spent on Christmas gifts for her family.

His voice had taken on a stern edge, the tone a reminder of the budget he had imposed, along with his suggestion for more economical gag gifts. The confrontation soon swelled into a full-blown dispute.

Finding her voice, Selena challenged Richard's judgment, reminding him that he placed no budget constraints on his own family. Selena's anger simmered beneath the surface. She was tired of his double standards, of his attempts to control her every move.

"Why is it okay for you to shower your family with expensive gifts," her voice rose, sharp with indignation, "but I'm expected to stick to a budget? It's not fair, Richard. You bought your mother a car for her 70th birthday!" she reminded him, her voice laced with defiance.

She recounted all the extravagant gifts he had bestowed upon his own family, while he expected her to give her family cheap gag gifts. She was tired of it. As the argument raged on, the air grew heavy with tension, the atmosphere saturated with escalating emotions.

Selena visibly saw her husband's face change, his eyes blazing red. She could see the disgust that he wasn't controlling her—his tactics no longer working.

In the grip of his furious rage, he struck her with a heavy hand. She felt like a battered child—unloved and always in trouble.

This isn't the way you treat a human being, she thought bitterly. That blow was meant to break me, to force me into submission... as if I were an animal to be tamed.

Gripping her aching face, she grappled with the question of how she had ended up with a man like this. She had never seen her father raise his hand to her mother or talk to her like she was nothing.

As she sat there staring into her vanity, making sure the bruise was all covered up, she realized she'd become a master of concealing her suffering.

What was she showing her daughter? Would she pick a man like this? Did Jordan see through her facade?

Walking out of the bathroom to find her sunglasses on the dresser, she looked over at Richard, engrossed in the digital receipts of her spending. He didn't even look over at her to see if she was okay. Then, in a panic, she realized Jordan might be back from the neighbor's house.

"Jordan!" she called out, her voice raspy. "Jordan, are you back?"

Disgust still evident, Richard glanced at her and informed her that he had called to check on Jordan, who was now at home packing the car with the gifts—gifts worth as much as their car payment. He then added that he wouldn't be going with them to the family Christmas party.

His call to check on Jordan—not her—fueled her irritation. But the news of his absence from the family Christmas Eve party filled her with anxiety. The question of how to explain his absence gnawed at her, but when she dared to ask, the flash of rage in his eyes confirmed her decision to escape before the situation worsened.

The car's tires hissed against the wet asphalt as Selena and her teenage daughter, Jordan, drove away from their neighborhood. The rhythmic thump of the windshield wipers punctuated the silence, each swipe a reminder of the storm brewing both outside and within.

Selena's knuckles turned white as she gripped the steering wheel, her hands trembling with the weight of unspoken words. The air was thick with the scent of Jordan's perfume—vanilla and lavender—a fragrance that somehow seemed out of place in the midst of so much uncertainty.

Jordan, of course, sensed her mother's tension. Selena, however, brushed it off, assuring her daughter that everything was fine. A few minutes of quiet reflection were all she needed, she said. To fill the silence of the 45-minute drive to her parents' house, she suggested they put on one of Jordan's playlists.

As they drove, Selena's thoughts drifted back to when her marriage started to change. It all began when she decided to enroll in online courses. At first, Selena viewed the courses as a simple distraction—a way to fill the empty hours between school runs. Little did she know that this seemingly harmless decision would ignite a passion within her that would change the course of her life.

Richard, the VP of HR at one of the biggest law firms in the city, initially appeared to welcome the idea. The world he inhabited dictated that she be the polished accessory at his side. Richard was on board with her studies and felt it would be a good look for him to have an accomplished wife.

As the virtual lectures played out on her screen and the digital pages of her e-books turned, she discovered an insatiable hunger for knowledge. It was as if she had found a hidden wellspring within herself that had long lain dormant.

The initial goal of escaping monotony soon blossomed into a commitment to her education. Selena's dedication and tireless effort led her along a path that eventually culminated in a doctorate degree.

This remarkable achievement opened doors for her in the world of philanthropy, where she was already a familiar face at charity events. Selena discovered not only a sense of purpose but also a renewed sense of self—her presence casting a new and radiant glow upon their union as she stood beside Richard.

Ironically, as Selena's star rose in academia, Richard's attempts to dim her light intensified. He grew resentful of the attention she garnered, vehemently opposing her use of the title "Doctor."

Among her friends in the charity world, she was proudly introduced as "Dr. Selena Bradford," a title that Richard could hardly bear. Unhappiness had become an unwelcome shadow in Selena's life, slowly distorting the woman she once was.

As the road stretched before her, the shadows cast by the streetlights across her face felt just like her life—light and dark, up and down, never steady. The passing miles rolled like a film of memories through her mind. The first twenty passed in silence, the low hum of the car's engine a reminder of the unspoken tension lingering in the air.

Breaking the silence, Jordan's hand reached out and gently squeezed her mother's shoulder—a silent gesture of understanding and support.

"Are you ready to talk, Mom?" Jordan's voice cut through the quiet of the car. Selena tried to feign ignorance, asking, "What are you talking about, Jordan?"

Her daughter, mature beyond her years, continued, "I know, Mom, and it's time for you and me to leave Dad and be safe. Do you hear me?"

Selena's breath caught in her throat, each sob a painful truth she had been carrying. For the next few minutes, they drove in silence, the weight of Jordan's words sinking in.

"Mom, you've been battered—not just physically but emotionally. I love Dad, just as much as you do, but it's time for us to breathe freely without fear. Will you trust me, Mom?"

Selena felt the tears welling up once more, not from sadness but from a glimmer of hope—a sense of courage that her daughter's words had ignited. She squeezed Jordan's hand and nodded, "Yes, baby, I trust you."

Jordan's voice was determined as she continued, "It's time for you to choose yourself, Mom."

Selena took a deep breath. Jordan's words were a life-line in the stormy sea of their lives, offering promise. "You're right, Jordan."

Jordan's eyes welled with tears as she confessed, "I heard your argument with Dad, and I know that he hit you." Her words hung heavy in the air—an unspoken truth finally given voice.

Selena's heart ached, realizing that her daughter had been privy to the pain and turmoil she had tried so desperately to keep hidden. But there was also a sense of relief in knowing that she was no longer alone. With a soft nod, Selena said, "Yes, he did."

"You should have seen the look in Dad's eyes," Jordan began, her voice trembling. "He almost looked like some kind of beast. But I stayed calm and packed the car, praying you'd come out so we could leave."

Jordan's eyes shone with a quiet resolve, her grip on her mother's hand firm. Selena gazed upon her child, seeing courage in her eyes.

"Let's pull over and pray, Mom," Jordan said.

Together, mother and daughter bowed their heads, entwined in prayer. Jordan's prayer was a soft murmur, filled with gratitude and a plea for protection. And as they prayed, the car filled with a sense of peace.

Jordan spoke softly, her voice shaking. "Mom, we shouldn't go home after the party. We could stay with Grandma and Grandpa until we figure things out."

Selena sat in the driver's seat, her hands gripping the steering wheel tight again, her mind racing, feeling the weight of her daughter's words.

The implications were immense. Moving out meant leaving behind not just a house, but a life—a life Selena had built with her husband. He might be what he is, but they lived a nice life.

As Jordan's voice trembled with emotion, Selena's heart ached. She wanted to shield her daughter from the harsh realities of their situation, but a decision this big had to be contemplated. They needed a carefully constructed plan.

However, Selena knew Jordan's suggestion wasn't just a whim. How could she deny her daughter's plea for safety?

So, with a heavy heart, Selena nodded, silently agreeing to Jordan's proposal.

Yet, amidst this acknowledgment, Selena couldn't help but feel torn. Her mind was a whirlwind of conflicting thoughts, unsure of what decision to make. Should she stay and try to mend what was broken, or should she heed Jordan's suggestion and seek solace elsewhere? The answer eluded her.

Just when she felt like someone finally understood, she felt lost and alone again.

CHAPTER THREE

SAM & PAULA

ECHOES OF CHANGE

The morning after the teachers' party felt like a victory lap as Sam surveyed the living room he and his wife were too tired to pick up the night before. Iridescent confetti sprinkles sparkled on the plush carpet, a half-empty sticky punch bowl sat on the foldout table, and the lingering scent of a sugar cookie candle mingled with the fresh pine needles from the Christmas tree.

Evidence of a job well done lay scattered amidst a sea of overturned glasses and ceramic plates. Paula, his partner in crime and in life, hummed a cheerful rendition of "Deck the Halls" as she straightened up pillows and smoothed out wrinkled cushions.

"That scavenger hunt was a stroke of genius, honey," Sam said, wrapping his arm around her waist and feeling the soft warmth of her Christmas pajamas beneath his fingers.

"The look on old Mr. Jenkins' face when he found that box of 'World's Best Teacher' pencils was priceless."

Paula laughed, a sound that always sent a flutter through Sam's heart. "Anything to keep those teachers on their toes. Besides," she winked, "they deserve a little fun after dealing with high school students all year."

Pride swelled in Sam's chest. The school where he was principal had just received the National School of Character Award, one of the highest honors they could receive. The teachers' Christmas party at his house was his way of saying thank you.

Snippets of conversations from the party replayed in his mind—the excitement over Secret Santa gifts, the shared jokes about lesson plans gone awry, the clinking of glasses filled with eggnog.

As Sam and Paula continued picking up the house before heading out to his family's Christmas party, Paula instructed Sam to get the family presents out of the closet to finish wrapping a few last-minute gifts.

The crinkle of wrapping paper filled the room as they worked, a familiar sound that always brought a sense of anticipation. Sam wasn't surprised when Paula confided her worries about his brother Bo and his now ex-wife Trinity's divorce.

"She'll always be my sister-in-law," she'd murmured, her eyes—normally sparkling—now reflecting the twinkling lights on the tree in a more subdued way. "It's going to feel weird seeing Bo and Josh without her."

Sam squeezed her hand, feeling a slight tremble in her fingers as the cold metal of her wedding ring rubbed against his skin. He understood the bond she and Trinity had as the only two sisters-in-law.

Life could change in an instant, and I fear we've all taken our blessings for granted, he thought, the truth echoing in the silence of the empty living room.

Heading to the laundry room to search for more wrapping tape, Sam felt a tug in his heart to do better checking in on his brother. Although they talked all the time, they hadn't really *really* talked.

As he rifled through the drawers, the metallic clatter of scissors and tape dispensers echoing in the small space, he thought about the look on Paula's face and knew it wasn't just about Bo and Trinity's divorce.

There's something more in her eyes—something unspoken. *Is it the weight of these changes, or a deeper longing
for home?*

As he walked back into the dining room where Paula
was wrapping the gifts, he decided to ask her gently.

"You okay, honey?" Sam asked, noticing her gaze fixed
on a distant corner of the room. She blinked, then smiled,
though the corners of her mouth didn't quite reach her
eyes.

"Just thinking about Mom's red velvet cake. Remember that year she accidentally put salt instead of sugar?"

Sam chuckled, the memory flooding back, briefly dis-
pelling the chill of worry. But beneath the laughter, he
knew there was more on Paula's mind.

As they finished wrapping the gifts, it was finally time
for them to head out to the family Christmas party. Sam
loaded up the car, slammed the trunk shut, and caught
Paula's gaze as she came out of the house.

The crunch of her footsteps on the Bermuda grass
was still heard despite the neighbors' children playing
outside. He watched as she crossed the yard, her winter coat pulled tight against the chill, a colorful scarf
wrapped around her neck. The sunlight glinted off the

rich, chocolate-brown strands of her hair. It highlighted the laugh lines around her eyes. Twenty-six years and a set of twins later, Paula still took his breath away.

Her smile, though still as warm as the day they met, appeared less often now that one twin was at college and the other was figuring out their next steps. This subtle shift in her demeanor made him realize that perhaps he and his wife had a few unspoken dreams.

It had been a few years into their lives as empty nesters, and Sam could feel the change. His hands tightened on the car keys, a knot of uncertainty forming in his stomach as he wondered where this new phase of their lives would lead them. When Paula reached the driver's side door, a playful smile tugging at her lips.

"You keep looking at me like that, and we'll end up back in the house."

Sam grinned, his heart skipping a beat as he chuckled and slid into the driver's seat, the warmth of the car a welcome contrast to the December chill.

"Remember the day we first met?"

Sam asked, recalling the flustered young woman who'd accidentally delivered a package to their doorstep.

Paula chuckled, her cheeks flushing with a rosy hue that hadn't faded after all these years. "How could I forget? I was such a klutz, dropping that box right at your feet."

"You couldn't take your eyes off me," he teased, enjoying the way her laughter filled the car.

"Well, who could blame me?" she retorted, a twinkle in her eye.

Sam often recalled how he witnessed the deep connection his parents shared growing up, and felt grateful to have found that same spark with Paula.

They'd built a life together, raised two amazing children, and now stood on the precipice of a new adventure. Although the empty nest had brought freedom, their newfound love for travel had become a source of both joy and subtle tension.

While they enjoyed exploring new places together, Sam couldn't deny the thrill he felt when he went off by himself, capturing the world through his camera lens. He felt invigorated—something he hadn't experienced in a long time as a high school principal.

While he was snapping photos of mountains and exotic plants, he realized it was more than a hobby. It was a passion that whispered of a different path—a life where he could trade meetings and schedules for the open road and the perfect shot.

Could this be my calling? he wondered silently, feeling the stir of possibilities.

But Sam had always been the responsible one. Doing something out of sheer want was something that never occurred to him. He always weighed all of the options and considered how decisions would affect the people he loved.

He found it peculiar that now, with the twins out of the house and life less busy, he spent a lot of time reflecting on the past and the future.

What would Paula think if he told her he wanted to be a professional photographer at 54? Would she see it as a midlife crisis, a foolish whim? Would his family raise their eyebrows? Would his friends give him skeptical looks?

As they drove toward his parents' house, listening to Christmas music on the radio, Sam glanced over at Paula, her profile illuminated by the bright glow of the sun streaming through the car windows.

The years had been kind to her, etching a few fine lines around her eyes and mouth, but her beauty remained radiant. Yet, there was a wistfulness in her expression, a hint of a longing that mirrored his own.

Perhaps, like him, she harbored dreams that remained unspoken. Maybe she, too, felt the pull of a different path—a desire to explore the uncharted territories of her own heart.

In her youth, Paula had been a head-turner, a young woman brimming with potential and the promise of endless possibilities. Sam knew it would take more than his good looks to allure a girl like her, and he was tired of surface relationships. He decided that with Paula, he wanted to show the depths of his character.

From the start, he respected her individuality, and Paula fell in love with his gentle spirit. Sam had offered her a life where she could be herself, and in Paula's eyes, that was worth more than any fleeting physical attraction.

However, married at eighteen, Paula had to embrace a different kind of beauty—one that blossomed from shared dreams and a loving partnership. She chose a life where her roles as wife and mother took center stage.

As Sam embarked on his journey through education, culminating in a doctorate, Paula had been his steadfast support. She helped him lay the foundation of a career

that would later become a cornerstone of their life together.

In those early years, Sam watched as Paula relished her
role as a homemaker, finding joy in caring for their twins,
Angela and Angel. She was the epitome of a devoted wife,
often seen at Sam's school gatherings, warmly greeting
guests and contributing to the betterment of the school
and community.

She was the quintessential soccer mom, the ballet
mom, the one who lovingly prepared lunches and baked
cupcakes for school events. Her name was synonymous
with their neighborhood and Sam's school.

Now, with the children having left the nest and Sam
comfortably established in his career, he observed a shift
in Paula. The years of selfless dedication were giving way
to a newfound sense of self. Paula was deep into her
newfound hobbies and personal pursuits.

Although he was happy to finally see his wife do something for herself, at times it felt like her desire for independence was slowly eclipsing their relationship. Sam
wanted to share his feelings about this growing space,
but he was afraid that once these concerns were spoken
aloud, they might take on a life of their own.

Their togetherness was changing, and it wasn't unusual for them to venture off separately during their travels, indulging in activities that piqued their individual interests.

Yet, at the end of each day, they always came back together, sharing stories of their excursions over dinner and engaging in discussions that, for the moment, seemed to bridge the gap. However, Sam often noticed how Paula seemed to gravitate toward solitude.

He understood that it wasn't that her love for him had diminished; it was simply that she had finally found some liberty. He observed her as she became the storyteller, recounting her adventures to him—just as he had done coming home from work with tales from his workplace.

Sam could see the concern on his own face reflected in Paula's eyes when she noticed his unease at her need for independence. But she reassured him that as long as they shared their experiences, their marriage would thrive.

Ironically, just as their lives were subtly diverging, the lives of their children—once inseparable twins—were also taking unexpected turns.

Angela, driven by her dream of becoming a pediatrician, was filled with a sense of purpose as she pursued her compassionate calling.

Angel, on the other hand, ventured into the uncertain realm of entrepreneurship, fueled by a burning passion to forge his own path as a business owner.

Sam also observed how his wife wasn't entirely supportive of Angel's career choice, and it was beginning to cause some discord. At family gatherings, he observed her overt pride in Angela's achievements, coupled with a subtle disregard for Angel's aspirations.

For now, he'd choose to sit with his observations and not let his worry deepen as they neared his parents' home—although in the back of his mind, he feared that Paula's favoritism toward Angela would once again rear its ugly head.

Chapter Four

LISA

Roses & Reservations

As Lisa carefully poured a can of 7Up into the batter of her pound cake, she couldn't help but smile as she felt the gentle breeze wafting through the open windows, carrying with it the unmistakable scent of salt and sea from the nearby ocean. Her new home, a cozy haven not far from the beach, embraced her with its coastal charm and soothing ambiance.

After years of dedication and perseverance in her career as a sports journalist, Lisa had finally reached the pinnacle of success.

After years of chasing deadlines and rewriting the rules of the game, I finally get to call this place home, she thought, a quiet pride warming her heart.

The fruits of her labor had granted her the luxury of this tranquil retreat—a sanctuary where she could unwind and savor the rewards of her hard work.

The coastal decor of her home reflected her love for the sea, with hues of aqua blues and sandy beige adorning the walls, complemented by driftwood accents and seashell motifs scattered throughout.

The airy living room boasted oversized windows that invited the sunlight to dance across the hardwood floors, casting warm, inviting shadows.

As Lisa delicately slid her pound cake into the warm oven, the familiar fragrances of vanilla intertwined with the tangy notes of lemon and lime enveloped her nautical kitchen.

Baking was her sanctuary—a form of therapy, a way to center herself amidst the chaos of life. It was her haven, especially in moments when she needed to brace herself for the whirlwind of emotions that awaited her at family gatherings.

Her mind drifted to thoughts of her sister, Selena, their relationship fraught with complexities that lingered like a shadow, casting a subtle weight on Lisa's shoulders. Her relationship with her only sister had always been fraught with drama, a constant undercurrent in Lisa's life.

Last Christmas's trivial conflict over tamales echoed in her mind, creating a sense of apprehension about what might transpire this year.

Her brother Bo's call, emphasizing a drama-free gathering, resonated deeply, and Lisa was determined to navigate the evening without stirring the pot—to keep the peace amidst the storm of familial tensions.

Just as she was getting ready to set the timer for her cake, her phone rang unexpectedly, disrupting her thoughts.

As Lisa's phone buzzed with Liam Grayson's name on the caller ID, a soft smile crept onto her lips. His warm wishes for a Merry Christmas echoed through the line, filling her heart with a gentle warmth.

She had grown accustomed to athletes reaching out to her, a side effect of her career as a sports journalist—but Liam was different.

In the whirlwind of her past marriage to a professional athlete, Lisa had experienced the highs and lows of life in the fast lane. The road trips, the adoring fans, the complex dynamics of stepchildren and multiple mothers—it was a world that had once overwhelmed her, leaving her feeling lost and unable to keep pace with its demands.

But amidst the chaos, there was no bitterness lingering within her heart despite the tumultuous journey that had led to her divorce. Lisa had found peace within herself. And in Liam, she found something unexpected—a genuine connection that transcended the superficiality she had grown accustomed to.

Their friendship had blossomed gradually, forged through countless conversations both on and off the court. Unlike the flirty and arrogant players she had encountered in the past, Liam exuded a kindness and respect that touched her deeply.

He saw her not just as another member of the sports world, but as a person worthy of genuine friendship and respect. In their conversations, hours would slip away as they delved into topics ranging from the mundane to the profound. He listened without judgment, offering support and companionship in a way that felt truly sincere.

As Liam's confession hung in the air, Lisa felt a rush of emotions surge. The revelation that he had sought out her address through her best friend Nanji initially sparked a flicker of apprehension within her.

Yet, as Liam elaborated on the reason behind his actions—a special delivery—her curiosity was ignited. With cautious steps, Lisa approached her front door, her pulse quickening with anticipation.

As she turned the handle and pushed the door open, she was met with a sight that took her breath away—a breathtaking display of vibrant blooms sprawled across her lawn, emitting an intoxicating floral fragrance that enveloped her senses.

In awe, Lisa's gaze traced the elegant arrangement, her heart skipping a beat as she read the message spelled out in delicate petals:

"Please Go Out With Me."

Speechless, Lisa stepped onto her lawn and found herself surrounded by the breathtaking beauty of the floral display. The gesture—so thoughtful and romantic—touched her deeply. For the first time in a long while, she felt cherished, valued, and desired... a feeling she had longed for, but never dared to believe would be hers.

The contrast between the weight of strained family ties and the unexpected sweetness of Liam's gesture overwhelmed her. In the midst of her worries and uncertainties, here was a man who had orchestrated an elaborate display to win her heart.

The transition from nervousness about her sister to the tantalizing romantic intrigue of Liam was like stepping out of a shadow into sunlight.

Lost in the moment, Lisa stood amidst the sea of roses, savoring the sweetness of the gesture and allowing herself to be swept away by the enchantment of it all. As Lisa basked in the beauty of the moment, her senses were suddenly jolted to attention at the alarming scent of smoke.

Panic surged through her veins as the realization hit her like a ton of bricks—she had forgotten all about her pound cake in the oven.

Her heart raced as she dashed back into the house, fear gnawing at her as she flung open the door to reveal the charred remains. Plumes of smoke billowed out, a stark reminder of the distraction caused by Liam's surprise delivery.

With a heavy sigh of relief that her kitchen wasn't engulfed in flames, Lisa gingerly retrieved the burnt cake, her frustration mounting at the realization of her forgetfulness. Just as she was attempting to salvage what was salvageable, her phone rang once more, interrupting her frantic efforts.

Without bothering to check the caller ID, she answered hastily, her voice tinged with haste.

"Sir, I'm about to burn my house down because of you."

On the other end of the line, her best friend Nanji's hearty laughter echoed through the receiver.

"Is that so, my dear?"

Nanji's voice was laced with amusement, her easygoing charm shining through even over the phone. Rolling her eyes, Lisa couldn't help but grin.

"I've got a bone to pick with you, Nanji. I can't believe you gave Liam my address."

But Nanji's laughter was infectious, washing away Lisa's worries and filling her with a sense of joy and excitement.

It was clear that her friend had orchestrated something truly special, and Lisa couldn't help but feel touched by the effort.

"How did you like the roses?"

Nanji's question was filled with anticipation, the intensity in her voice a clear sign of her dedication to making this unforgettable for her dear friend. Her creativity, along with the florist's, had woven deep reds and delicate whites—each rose handpicked to symbolize the profound depth of Liam's admiration. The result was a breathtaking sight that would sweep Lisa off her feet.

Lisa's smile danced through her words.

"Oh, Nanji, they're absolutely stunning! I can hardly believe Liam went through all this effort. It's the most beautiful thing anyone has ever done for me. It was like a scene from a romance movie."

Lisa couldn't help but chuckle, appreciating her friend's role in orchestrating this extraordinary gesture.

"I knew you'd love it. They say when a man puts in that much effort, he's truly smitten. What do you think? Could this be the beginning of something beautiful for you?"

With a mixture of emotions, Lisa chuckled, "Well, he is charming, and the roses certainly left an impression. But you know my rule about athletes."

Nanji, undeterred, expressed her confidence. "You two would be perfect for each other. He's crazy about you."

Lisa was amused by her friend's enthusiasm but remained firm. "You know dating another athlete is out of the question. I've been there and done that."

"Well, my dear," Nanji replied, "this guy seems very persistent. He's not going down without a fight. It's not every day you encounter someone who goes to such lengths to show their genuine interest."

Her words held a mixture of excitement and curiosity as she pondered the unfolding romance. In their conversation, Lisa didn't reveal the fluttering in her heart when Liam told her he'd await her answer next year. She appreciated the respect he had shown by not pressuring her to give an answer immediately.

As Lisa wrapped up the call with Nanji and glanced at the clock, she breathed a sigh of relief knowing she had ample time to whip up a fresh pound cake for the party, despite the earlier setback.

As she began to gather the ingredients and mix them together, the delightful aroma filled her kitchen, quickly dissipating the lingering scent of smoke and restoring a sense of warmth and comfort.

With the new batter safely placed in the oven, Lisa took a moment to step outside onto her front lawn again.

She paused to admire the exquisite beauty of the roses once more, their delicate petals unfolding gracefully in a mesmerizing display.

"How beautiful," she whispered, her heart swelling with gratitude and warmth.

It served as a tangible reminder that amid life's chaos and complexities, God has the power to inspire someone to do something truly extraordinary for you.

Standing there, deeply moved, Lisa couldn't help but marvel at the unexpected surprise that had come her way. Liam's gesture had left an indelible mark on her heart, reminding her of the beauty of human connection and the power of love.

But now, faced with the dilemma of how to bring all the beautiful flowers into her home, Lisa pondered her next move. Before she could come up with a plan, another flower delivery truck pulled up, its driver greeting her with a smile.

"Ms. Franklin, now that you've seen the message, where would you like us to put your roses?" the driver asked.

A wide smile graced Lisa's lips as she realized that Liam had paid attention to even the smallest details.

"The backyard will do just fine," she replied with gratitude.

And so, just as the thought of Liam Grayson had found a special place in her heart, the roses found a special place in Lisa's backyard—in front of her favorite window where she liked to sit and pray.

CHAPTER FIVE

BO

THE FIRST CHRISTMAS ALONE

The department store pulsed with Christmas cheer. Garlands dripped from the ceiling, tinsel glittered on every corner, and carols blared from unseen speakers. But the festive overload only made Bo's loneliness sharper. He navigated the aisles like a stranger in a strange land, each happy couple a painful reminder of what he'd lost.

For 19 years, Trinity had been his partner in creating cherished Christmas memories. She had been the heart of their family's traditions—gift choices, favorite dishes, bringing smiles to the faces of their loved ones.

And now, as Bo navigated through the aisles, he felt so empty, still in disbelief that he was choosing gifts for the family gathering. It felt so foreign. His ex-wife had always handled all of this. Buying gifts for everyone felt so trivial.

How could Trinity allow this to happen to their family? Or perhaps, how could he let things reach this point? The lines between blame and self-reproach blurred in his mind.

Trinity's absence loomed large, a gaping hole that seemed impossible to fill. They had been through so much together, and her influence in his life was immeasurable. The debate raged within him as he contemplated whether to call her, angrily throwing an item he had chosen into the cart.

He questioned his own independence and ability to step into a role he had never occupied. And then, in a moment of vulnerability, he closed his eyes and let out a deep sigh as his fingers dialed Trinity's number.

Trying to control his underlying anger, he rolled his eyes and looked at the phone, annoyed when she didn't answer after the first couple of rings. When the call finally connected, Bo couldn't help but feel a mix of emotions—Trinity's voice was familiar and comforting.

Anger, love, and relief filled the line, but so did a heavy weight of remorse that rested upon his shoulders. She didn't have to answer, but she did. Trinity was still there for him, even after everything.

"I don't know what to get the nieces and nephews this year. You always knew exactly what to pick."

Trinity, in her ever-understanding way, began offering suggestions, walking him through the aisles of the store over the phone. She reminded him not to forget the wrapping paper and some tape—a simple act of love he would have definitely overlooked.

As she guided him through the shopping, he couldn't help but remember the years leading up to their separation. The long hours he had devoted to his career had often taken precedence over the time he should have spent with Trinity and their son, Josh.

Her grievances had piled up like heavy stones, and she'd repeatedly expressed how it felt like she was a married woman leading a single life.

As the sales clerk led him to the latest trendy purses Trinity suggested for his nieces, he shook his head, remembering the countless designer bags he'd had his secretary buy for Trinity through the years. He thought of the money he spent on cars, jewelry, expensive spa retreats—but still, complaint after complaint.

Although he'd reached his relentless pursuit as a healthcare administrator, it had taken a toll on their marriage. He had been blind to her pain and deaf to her pleas, distracted by the pursuit of what he thought was best for their family.

Then one day, after years of feeling like a solitary entity, Trinity made the fateful decision. While on vacation with their son, she informed Bo that she wouldn't be returning. The words had hit him like a freight train, and he realized, with painful clarity, that he had lost her.

In the aftermath, Bo had tried to make amends, to do the things she had longed for—the simple acts of shared time and the affection she craved. But it was too late. Trinity's heart had already shifted, and the damage was irreparable.

The bond that once held them together had unraveled before his very eyes. Now he stood on the other side of their separation, piecing together the fragments of his shattered family.

Bo's remorse was a constant companion, as guilt enveloped him. He knew he had been unfair during the divorce as well, like fighting for the house. Why should she have it when it was the very place she had chosen to leave? Bo had also contested alimony, a decision he couldn't help but view as unjust in hindsight.

Yet, despite the turmoil, he acknowledged his immense luck in maintaining a good relationship with Trinity. She had always been mature, even in the midst of their separation.

Their son Josh, a wise and remarkably mature fifteen-year-old, believed his parents were better off apart. His son had become a life coach, guiding him through the landscape of their altered family dynamics. Josh spoke truth with the clarity only a child could possess. He emphasized that Trinity didn't hate him, and they needed to be friends.

As Bo paid for the gifts and patronized a Girl Scout troop wrapping gifts outside the department store, he felt a little nervous. He knew the eyes of his family would be upon him, judging his actions, and he anticipated the snide comments he knew would surface.

Trinity had been the best thing that ever happened to him, and this Christmas would be the first without her. As he gathered the gifts in the car and made his way to pick up Josh, his mind wandered back to their wedding day.

The memory now stung and hurt him deeply. He could still picture her radiant smile as she walked down the aisle with her father. But now, as he pulled into the driveway of her house, he watched her emerge with their son, and that same smile felt like a cruel reminder of times past.

The realization hit him like a sledgehammer to the chest—he had been the architect of his own downfall. His foolish pride and stubbornness had driven a wedge between them. As he gazed upon her, he couldn't help but marvel at her resilience. She was still the same beautiful woman he had fallen in love with.

And yet, beneath the facade of strength, he sensed her vulnerability and knew he'd hurt her deeply. He knew that if he couldn't find a way to mend their broken bond, someone else would gladly step into his shoes.

The thought cut him to the core, igniting a fire within him to fight for what was rightfully his. They greeted each other with a warm hug, their silent pain for one another evident.

Bo's heart sank with a sense of longing as her hair brushed against his nose, filling him with the scent of her fragrance. Her big beautiful brown eyes sparkled against her white sweater as she wore his favorite pair of blue jeans.

Every time he saw her, he realized how much he had taken for granted, and how deeply he still cared. Trinity, radiant and composed, always captivated Bo from the first time he saw her at church.

When Trinity expressed her sadness at not attending the Christmas party, Bo's heart sank. Their exchange was fraught with unspoken truths hanging heavy in the air. She told him how Lila and Henry, gracious as ever, had extended an invitation, and his sisters had reached out with kindness, but Trinity declined, telling him time was needed. Trinity waved goodbye, and just as quickly as he got a glimpse of her, she was back inside her house.

As father and son drove off, Josh adjusted the volume down on the radio, acknowledging the discomfort that hung in the air.

"That was awkward."

Mature beyond his years, Bo knew the chemistry and air between them was so thick even a baby could sense it.

"Was it that obvious?" Bo said, knowing his son was keen to it all. Josh offered his father a small but reassuring smile.

"Mom needs time to just be herself, and you need time to reflect."

Stung by his son's wisdom, Bo knew he was right and marveled at how he'd become a guiding light for both him and Trinity.

With a mixture of pride and humility, Bo absorbed Josh's words. Time, as Josh pointed out, was the key to healing wounds that ran deep.

Yet, amidst the turmoil of his emotions, there was a glimmer of hope. Despite agreeing that time heals all wounds, Bo was resolute in his determination to win Trinity back—before someone else did.

CHAPTER SIX

SELENA &
JORDAN

UNVEILED SECRETS

At the stop sign, Selena felt a deep sense of connection as she turned into her old neighborhood. The once-vivid colors of the houses—soft blues, cheerful yellows, and warm beiges—seemed to glow in the afternoon light.

Tall palm trees, their leaves rustling in the breeze, lined the streets, casting dappled shadows on the neatly trimmed lawns. Each house, with its unique charm, evoked memories, making every corner of the neighborhood hold special significance.

As she drove past the golf course, her gaze landed on a weathered park bench tucked beneath an old elm tree.

The bench, painted a faded green and dotted with peeling paint, had seen better days.

It reminded her of a first kiss shared with someone from her teenage years. She smiled as memories came flooding back—walking to her friend's house after school, the laughter of learning to skate in the cul-de-sacs, borrowing milk for Momma from a nearby church friend, and the camaraderie of helping with community yard sales.

Each memory was a vivid reminder of the carefree days that had shaped her—moments that seemed small then but now felt like the foundation of a life that had somehow drifted away.

She reflected on how much life had changed. Her teenage daughter rarely went outside, choosing instead to spend time on the computer or her cell phone. She shook her head, thinking about how different things were now.

Growing up, she knew everyone in her neighborhood; they looked out for each other. Now, she barely spoke to her neighbors, and instead of the community watch, everyone relied on their Ring home security systems.

Shaking her head, she marveled at the twists and turns life took. She wondered if her husband Richard felt any remorse. It took her by surprise that he hadn't even tried to call and apologize or say, "I'm sorry." After all, he saw her eye was bruising, and this was the first time in years he would miss the family Christmas gathering.

How could he do this? And what about all the questions that would come her way about his whereabouts? She couldn't lie and say he had to work—he was the boss and made the rules. They'd never spent a holiday apart. This was going to look really bad, and she hadn't even figured out what to say.

As they pulled into her parents' driveway, the familiar sight of the house brought a surge of mixed emotions to Selena. The stately two-story home, with its smooth tan exterior and crisp black trim, stood proud against the golden afternoon sky—just as it had for decades. The warm glow from the windows made it feel alive, as if the house itself had been waiting for them.

But it was the Christmas decorations that truly transformed it. Twinkling blue lights traced every eave and windowpane, casting a magical shimmer over the entire facade. Even the grand oak tree beside the house sparkled, its limbs wrapped in glowing strands that made it look like something out of a snow globe.

Selena's parents had become known in the neighborhood for their devotion to blue Christmas lights—a tradition born years ago when her father mistakenly purchased a box of only blue bulbs. What started as an accident had become a cherished family quirk, and now the house was a glowing beacon of blue every December. Selena took a deep breath, feeling the weight of her childhood memories press gently on her chest.

"We're going to get through this, Mom."

Her daughter's voice was a lifeline. Selena, heavy with guilt, found solace in Jordan's courage. With a mixture of sorrow and strength, they stepped out of the car and made their way to the house, the old wooden door creaking open to welcome them inside.

Selena cringed inwardly as Jordan blurted out, "Grand, Pops, I can't believe you still keep the door unlocked."

The warmth of the house enveloped her—a familiar mix of cinnamon potpourri, furniture polish, and pine needles from the Christmas tree. It was a scent that had once brought her comfort, but now it felt heavy, almost suffocating.

The grandfather clock in the corner ticked steadily, each second a reminder of the ticking time bomb that was her marriage. Lila and Henry, her parents, rose from their chairs, their faces creased with smiles that didn't quite reach their eyes.

"We don't have any secrets," Henry declared with a forced chuckle. Selena noticed the slight tremor in his hand as he reached out to hug her. *He knows something's wrong*, she thought.

"That's right," Lila chimed in, her gaze fixed on Jordan. "How's my Jordan?"

"I'm fine," Jordan replied, her voice barely above a whisper. Selena's heart ached for her daughter, the silent witness to her pain.

Henry, ever the protector, moved towards the door. "Let me go out here and show Richard where to park," he announced.

Panic fluttered in Selena's chest. "Oh, uhm, he's not going to make it today, Daddy." Her voice shook, and she clutched the pan of chili beans tighter, the warmth seeping through the thin dish towel.

"Take these chili beans into the kitchen, Jordan," Selena urged, desperate for a moment alone.

As Jordan disappeared into the kitchen, the familiar hum of the refrigerator filled the silence. Lila's eyes narrowed. "You soaked the beans this time, didn't you?"

"Yes ma'am," Selena mumbled, her throat tight. Henry chuckled, but the sound lacked its usual warmth.

"Your mother almost blew the roof off the place with that last pan of beans. Richard's not coming?"

Selena's escape route was forming. "No, he's not going to make it," she murmured. "Can I go to the room real quick?"

Without waiting for a response, she fled to the refuge of the spare bedroom, now a sewing room filled with the comforting scent of fabric and the small lavender sachets her mother kept under the chair cushions to keep her furniture smelling fresh.

I can't do this, she thought, her hands trembling.

She heard her mother's footsteps approaching.

"Mom, can I have just a minute alone?" Selena pleaded.

"Let me open the blinds," Lila said, her voice laced with concern.

"I just need a minute, Mom," Selena insisted, her fingers fumbling with the clasp of her sunglasses.

"I'm surprised to see you with sunglasses on. Don't they give headaches?" Lila's voice was gentle, but Selena could hear the unspoken question beneath it.

"Yes, ma'am," Selena lied, her voice barely a whisper.

Lila's cool fingers brushed against Selena's cheek as she gently removed the sunglasses. The room seemed to tilt, and Selena squeezed her eyes shut against the sting of the overhead light.

"You forgot to cut the tags off."

Selena's heart pounded in her chest. She scrambled through her purse, head down, praying for a miracle.

"Oh, I didn't even realize I didn't take the tag off," she stammered. "Just set them down when you cut the tag, Mom. I'll be right out to help you cook."

But Lila didn't move. Selena could feel her mother's gaze on her, burning into her skin. After a long pause, she looked up. Lila's face was a mask of shock and sorrow.

"Richard did this to you?" Lila's voice was barely a whisper, but it echoed in the small room.

The dam broke. Selena collapsed into her mother's arms, sobs wracking her body. "Richard has us on a tight budget, and he got upset about the money I spent on Christmas gifts."

Lila's embrace was warm and comforting, but it couldn't erase the pain. "Where was Jordan?"

"She was outside packing up the car," Selena choked out. "I can't believe he did this right before the party."

Lila's hand stroked Selena's hair. "Is this the first time he's hit you?"

Selena shook her head, tears streaming down her face. "No."

"What are you going to do?" Lila's voice was firm but filled with love.

Henry's voice boomed from the hallway, "Y'all alright in there?"

"We're fine, Henry," Lila called back, her voice steady.

Selena pulled away, wiping her tears. She reached for her sunglasses, the coolness a stark contrast to the burning pain around her eye. The bruise, already darkening in shades of red and purple, stretched from her cheekbone to her eyebrow.

"Mom, I better get in the bathroom and put some more makeup on this."

"Alright now, get yourself cleaned up. We'll get through this."

Selena nodded, her heart heavy. She left the room, the weight of her secret pressing down on her. As she walked down the hall, she heard the muffled sound of her father's laughter, followed by Jordan's soft giggle coming from the kitchen.

We'll get through this, Selena repeated to herself, but the words felt hollow. Somehow, we'll get through this.

Chapter Seven

About Richard

A Bouquet of Deceit

S elena, can you please come down to the lobby? You have a delivery," the voice on the intercom announced, pulling her away from her work. Who could be sending her something? A flicker of curiosity danced through her. With a resigned sigh, she pushed back from her desk, the smooth leather of her chair squeaking in protest.

As the elevator doors opened into the lobby, her eyes were met with a breathtaking sight. An array of beautiful red roses adorned the counter, their vibrant color and intoxicating fragrance filling the air. Selena's eyes widened as she approached the counter. The concierge smiled warmly and handed her the bouquet.

"These were just delivered for you, Ms. Franklin," the concierge said with a knowing grin, recognizing the magic of the moment.

Selena's fingers, trembling with excitement, immediately reached for the card attached to the bouquet, her heart fluttering like a butterfly's delicate wings. She read the words, her lips forming a soft smile as she absorbed the sentiment:

"You're the most beautiful woman I've ever seen."

It was a compliment that made her heart swell with joy and her cheeks blush in sheer delight. The security guard on duty couldn't help but interject, his eyes twinkling with amusement.

"Impressive," he remarked with a chuckle. "I like his style."

Selena, still beaming, nodded in agreement. "Me too."

The world around her dissolved into the beauty of the moment. With the bouquet cradled in her arms, she made her way back to her desk, the delicate scent of baby's breath and roses drawing curious glances and whispers of "Who's the lucky girl?" Coworkers stopped her in her path, showering her with compliments and inquiring about the sender of the breathtaking bouquet.

Selena graciously accepted the compliments, her heart swelling with happiness.

As she finally returned to her desk, she rummaged through her purse, searching for a business card she'd acquired just the day before. She recalled a chance encounter during lunch with a handsome stranger.

The memory played in her mind like a reel of film. They had exchanged glances, the magnetic pull between them undeniable. And then, a bold move that had taken her by surprise—he had approached just as she stepped outside the restaurant to leave. She remembered his words, spoken with confidence and charm:

"You're the most beautiful woman I've ever seen."

Selena, rarely taken aback, had responded with a gracious "thank you," casting a sly glance at her astonished friend who accompanied her to lunch often.

Tall, dark, and handsome, he introduced himself as Richard. The exchange had left her intrigued and flattered. When he handed her his business card and asked for hers, she accepted, feeling a sense of excitement and anticipation.

Their brief encounter had left her enchanted, and with the roses now on her desk, she knew her feelings had not been misplaced. With Richard's business card in hand, she picked up her phone, dialed the number printed on the card, and waited with bated breath.

"Hi, this is Richard," he answered.

"I just received three dozen beautiful roses. Why, thank you, Richard. They are absolutely stunning." Her heart raced as she spoke.

And so, with those words, their whirlwind romance began—a series of romantic gestures from Richard that would come to define his deception.

He was a successful HR vice president at a prominent law firm, a man of stature and means. Selena had never encountered a man quite like Richard, an enigma wrapped in charisma. He embodied her deepest desires: sexy, handsome, a man whose success was rivaled only by his exquisite taste.

With every gift, every romantic gesture, he ensnared her heart, skillfully crafting a captivating narrative that beckoned her into his world. Yet, concealed beneath that charming facade was a master manipulator, a maestro orchestrating a symphony of deceit.

His every move had been calculated, a carefully laid trail of breadcrumbs leading Selena deeper into his web.

His intentions were far from the love he professed; they were shadows of evil she had never anticipated.

One fateful evening, Richard orchestrated an enchanting night at a high-end restaurant. The ambiance exuded luxury, as he presented her with a diamond necklace, a glittering sign of his devotion. After the lavish dinner, he led her to a secluded vista, the city's lights twinkling below.

With tenderness, he took her hand, and his words, overflowing with sweetness, lured her further into his trap.

"Selena," he breathed, his voice saturated with emotion, "I love you more than life itself. Will you do me the honor of becoming my wife?"

"Yes," she murmured, her voice a soft whisper. "I will, I will."

He slipped the diamond ring onto her finger, and with his kiss—just like a demonic spell—he was binding her to him with passion and promises. But beneath the facade of love, a hidden reality lurked.

Richard's charming overtures were merely a veil to obscure the darkness that festered within. He was a cold-hearted wolf masquerading as a lamb, and Selena, blinded by her own lust and dreams, was soon to discover that not all that glitters is gold.

In the dimly lit bathroom of her parents' house, Selena slipped off her shoes, the chill of the bathroom tiles seeping through her Christmas socks as she stared at her reflection in the mirror, the light casting shadows under her tired eyes.

As she gingerly dabbed foundation over her black eye, a sharp sting rippled through her skin, forcing her to wince. The familiar scent of her mother's lavender soap offered some soothing comfort, but even that couldn't soften the weight of the secrets she carried.

She remembered the advice given by her kind-hearted boss, Wes, back when she had introduced Richard at a Christmas party with her colleagues.

"How are things going with your new beau?" Wes inquired, returning from work the Monday after the Christmas party.

"Take it slow, Selena. Sometimes a man with means can come with a lot. You're young and vibrant. Give it some time before making any major decisions to move forward."

The advice Wes had imparted lingered like a silent echo, a pearl of wisdom she would recall on several occasions when doubts began to gnaw at her heart.

His words had been her first audible sign, the subtle tug of intuition urging her to pause and see beyond Richard's facade. But then, just as the shadows of doubt began to take root, Richard would weave a new strand of enchantment. He had a talent for sweeping her off her feet, a way of countering those inner warnings.

Not long after they married, Richard's control gradually took hold, starting with the unrelenting calls that invaded her everywhere she went. The demands for details about every conversation she had with family and friends. Selena was flattered at first, believing it was a sign of his devotion, his desire to be an integral part of her world.

But then the physical abuse began. It started with small pinches over trivial things like coming later than she reported after shopping or visiting with her parents too long, leaving her bruised.

Each episode was followed by Richard's remorse, tears in his eyes, and a masterful display of affection—cars, luxurious homes, expensive jewelry, and furs—all used as cloaks to hide the scars beneath.

The aftermath of the violence was a twisted intimacy. After his outbursts, when the self-loathing momentarily flickered in his eyes, they'd cling to each other on the bed or couch. It was a disturbing closeness, like a predator guarding its captured prey.

And somehow, like a nurturing woman clinging to fairy tale dreams, she forgave him time after time. This tendency intensified after Jordan's birth. Her longing for a stable family, mirroring her own upbringing, intertwined with Richard's ability to provide a lavish lifestyle.

She couldn't fathom any other way to raise her child, and the periodic breaks when Richard was out of town for work became her moments of respite. But now, with 16 years of secrets and suffering behind her, Selena knew it was time to confront her truth.

As she gazed at her reflection, she struggled to make a decision. The idea of moving back in with her parents, seeking their love and protection, was tempting. But would she find the strength to make this Christmas party the last one where she hid her pain? The diamond ring on her finger felt heavy, a symbol of both promise and possession. If only she had known...

Selena traced the bruise on her cheekbone, a stark reminder of Richard's true nature. A man who controlled her finances, monitored her every move, and lashed out in anger when she dared to defy him.

Tears welled up in her eyes as she reached for her sunglasses, the muffled voices of Jordan and her parents drifting from the kitchen. Guilt twisted in her stomach. She had always been the strong one, the one who held it all together. What would people think if they knew the truth?

I have to do something, she thought, her voice a silent plea. *For Jordan. For myself.*

But as she stepped back into the hallway, doubt crept in. *Could she really leave? Could she break free from the gilded cage Richard had built around her? Risk shattering the image she had carefully cultivated?* The answer remained elusive, suspended somewhere between her fear and her newfound resolve.

Chapter Eight

SAM & PAULA

The Crossroads of Tradition

Wrapped in the car's warmth, Sam and Paula shared smiles as the holiday radio station played their favorites. The car's heated seats added that extra layer of comfort. Outside, the sea of businesses and houses seen from the freeway transformed the landscape into a Christmas wonderland.

As they traversed the winding road, Sam's voice—warm and resonant—broke the comfortable silence as he began to share stories of his upbringing. He spoke of his parents' devotion to their faith and the strictness that filled their home. Paula's eyes sparkled with interest as she listened intently, her gloved hand resting gently on his arm.

Lila and Henry, Sam explained, had fashioned his world within the confines of their church. Deeply religious, there was no room for "the devil's music," no trips to the movies, no attending dances—not even the cherished high school prom.

Sam chuckled softly, recalling the forbidden allure of the latest tunes he had to muffle, filtering the sounds through his bedroom window. He even recalled the day he got whupped when his mother caught him doing the moonwalk in the backyard.

"The moonwalk?" Paula asked, laughing heartily. "Come on, did you have to pick the switch she spanked you with?" They both laughed hysterically. Sam and Paula had both grown up going to the backyard, picking the thinnest switch they'd get spanked with.

As they shared these stories they both already knew, Paula reminded Sam of her polar opposite upbringing—marked by an abundance of worldly experiences and indulgence in life's pleasures.

The taste of champagne at age thirteen, the thrill of music and all the latest dance moves, the rowdy crowds at the movies yelling at the characters—these were the memories that had painted her youth.

"You know, Sam," her voice carried the warmth of her found faith, "as much fun as I had, I sometimes wish I had been raised with the gift of Jesus in my life like you."

Sam remembered how rough it was when they first met freshman year in college. He was ready to get out there and do his thing—experience all the things he was brought up not to do. But when he met Paula, she had already found her way to the church. Her journey to spirituality gave him a strong sense of self-acceptance and a greater understanding of sacred life.

Although he had moved away from the strict confines of his upbringing, he understood those were man-made preferences, not requirements for heaven. Paula's faith strengthened his own and kept him within the church walls.

Paula turned to Sam, her eyes filled with humor. "I used to think your mother was so mean," her laughter echoing in the car's interior. Sam joined in, the shared memories warming the space between them. He recalled how his mom used to view Paula as a worldly influence.

"You know Momma thought you were worldly," he said, his voice filled with amusement. "She would say, 'That girl's dresses are too short.'"

Paula's laughter bubbled up again. "Your mom was vigilant, always offering me a hanky to drape over my knees."

"Their ways were so judgmental and harsh," Sam remarked, a hint of wistfulness in his voice.

"I think things would have been easier if they had just given me a chance to learn about God first. Then I would have naturally adopted modesty," Paula replied.

Sam, ever the voice of reason, reminded her that those were the ways of their time—a reflection of the culture and norms that prevailed.

"Yes," Paula agreed, a thoughtful smile gracing her lips. "You only do what you know. I love your mother now, but in the beginning, I was like, 'God, help me.'"

As their conversation meandered, Paula shifted in her seat, her eyes gleaming with excitement.

"I can't wait to see Angela and Angel at the party," she mused, her voice bright with anticipation.

The hum of the car engine and the soft rhythm of holiday music created a serene atmosphere, but an underlying tension lingered. Sam glanced out the window, watching the glow of Christmas lights blur past them.

"I wonder if your son is going to bring his little girl-friend," Paula said with a teasing smile.

Sam chuckled, shaking his head. He stole a glance at Paula, noting how her lips curved into that same amused smirk his mother used to wear. The similarity struck him like a familiar melody.

"You know," his voice playful but edged with irony, "you were just complaining about how my momma treated you. And now, you're doing the same thing to Angel's girlfriend."

Paula turned toward him, eyes wide in mock surprise. "This is different, Sam," she said lightly, though defensiveness crept in.

"Oh, really? How so?" Sam asked, a soft laugh escaping as he kept his hands steady on the wheel.

Their banter continued as they wove through familiar streets, the houses glowing in shades of red, green, and gold. But Sam couldn't shake the weight of what was happening between his wife and son—the quiet favoritism that lingered, the kind of tension often felt but rarely spoken aloud.

In the silence between their words, Sam let out a slow breath, feeling a knot in his chest. He turned to Paula.

"Babe, there's something I've been meaning to discuss with you."

Her playful expression faded. She shifted in her seat, her eyes searching his. The scent of peppermint from her lip balm mingled with the cool, crisp air.

"I've noticed something," Sam's voice tinged with uncertainty. "It's been on my mind for a while."

"What is it, Sam?" she asked gently, her hand reaching for his arm.

"Sometimes," he began, "I feel like you're showing favoritism with the twins."

She blinked. Silence stretched between them. Sam pressed on.

"You're incredibly proud of Angela—and you should be. She's becoming a doctor. But Angel—he's making strides too. His car wash business... it's going to take off."

Paula nodded, her eyes distant. "I'm proud of him, Sam. I just want him to reach his full potential."

"I get that," Sam said. "But maybe the way you push him... it feels like pressure."

"I only push him because I love him," she whispered. "I want him to see what I see in him."

Sam nodded. "I know. But sometimes love means letting them find their own path."

A heavy silence fell. Then Paula sat more upright. Sam felt it—he was bracing himself.

"I'd like to go on a trip by myself," she said, the words rehearsed.

They hit Sam like cold water.

"Why by yourself? This is our time."

"It would only be for a few days," she said. "I just. .. I need to explore what it's like to be with my own thoughts."

"When?" he asked.

"New Year's Eve."

Sam's heart clenched. "You want to spend New Year's Eve alone?"

"Yes," she said, resolute.

"Enough is enough," Sam said, trembling. "I've given you your space during vacations—that should be enough."

But Paula's eyes flashed. She turned fully toward him.

"First of all, you didn't 'let' me do anything. I'm not your child."

Sam was stunned. She continued.

"I considered you when I put my dreams on hold. When I stayed home with the kids while you earned your degrees. When I managed the household so you could study. Every choice I made—I made with you and the family in mind." Her voice rose. The heater now felt suffocating.

For ten minutes, they rode in silence.

Finally, Sam got off at the next exit and pulled over. Said nothing. Just held out his hand.

Paula bit her lip, stared into his eyes. Their fingers intertwined.

"I'm sorry, Paula. I guess I'm just uncomfortable with this," Sam whispered. "But everything I've ever wanted to do, you've supported. And now... it's your turn."

CHAPTER NINE

BO & JOSH

BRIDGES OF LOYALTY & LOVE

B o pushed open the backyard gate, the creak of the hinges breaking the quiet hum of winter air. Josh trailed just behind him, hoodie up, hands stuffed in his pockets. The scent of barbecue drifted toward them—smoky, familiar, and laced with something Bo hadn't smelled in a while: comfort.

Across the yard, he spotted his father at the grill, Lila by his side. The two stood close, talking low, heads tilted in that way couples do when the words carry weight. Bo slowed, catching a flash of something in Henry's eyes. Worry. He hated that look on his father.

As they stepped onto the patio, Bo caught just enough to ask what he overheard.

"So... Richard didn't come with Selena?"

Bo spotted the flicker in his parents' eyes—some silent exchange between them that he didn't quite catch but felt all the same. He knew what it was. This was the first time he'd shown up without Trinity, and it hung in the air like smoke off the grill.

They didn't answer his question about Richard. Bo noticed—but let it go. For now.

Still, his mother put on that smile of hers, the one that smoothed everything over.

"Look at you two—you look great," she said, like it was any other year. Bo appreciated the grace in that, more than she knew. His father, not one to dance around the truth, cut in.

"You'd look even better if Trinity was with you," Henry said, his tone just sharp enough to sting.

Bo flinched but didn't argue. He caught the way his mom glanced at Henry—warning in her eyes—and the way she gently said his name like it carried weight.

"Henry."

"I'm working on it," Bo said, jaw clenched. That was the most he could offer without unraveling right there on the patio.

Josh, standing close, jumped in before things got too tense. "Mom's doing fine, Grandpa," he said casually, but Bo saw the way his son looked up at him—curious, uncertain, maybe even a little worried.

Henry, never known for subtlety, let out a huff. "Boy, your dad really messed that up."

Bo braced himself, but it was his mom who stepped in first.

"We already talked about this, Henry," she said, firm.

Bo gave a quick nod. "I get it, Mom," he said quietly. He did. It was strange being here without Trinity. Everything felt... off.

Josh chuckled lightly, trying to ease the moment, and Bo was grateful for it. Then he watched as Lila turned her attention to Josh, her face softening with affection.

"Grandson, you're getting so tall," she said, already pulling the mood forward. "Come join me in the kitchen. Your cousin Jordan's here."

As they disappeared inside, Bo couldn't help but address his father. "I'm going to get her back," he said, alluding to Henry's remarks about Trinity.

Henry, with a wisdom born of experience, leaned in to offer his son a crucial insight.

"And that's where you got it all wrong, son. You have to fix you before you go trying to get a woman back."

Feeling the need to change the subject, Bo redirected the conversation.

"What's up with Richard?" he asked, steering the focus away from the lingering concern about his situation.

Henry, mindful of the sensitive nature and reluctant to reveal too much, chose his words carefully.

"Selena and Jordan are here, but Richard couldn't make it," he said, offering a cryptic explanation that hinted at deeper troubles.

Bo's reaction was less than subtle, punctuated with a touch of sarcasm.

"Mr. Rich Man didn't make it," he remarked.

Bo had never been fond of Selena's husband, viewing him as an arrogant figure who held himself above others. Richard's wealth and status had done little to improve his image in Bo's eyes.

But it was Bo's next revelation that truly caught Henry by surprise.

"You know Selena and Lisa haven't spoken for almost six months," Bo shared, his tone heavy with frustration.

"What?" Henry's eyebrows shot up in surprise.

"What's going on with those two?"

Bo shook his head. "Honestly, Dad, those two are always fighting. You know how judgmental Selena is."

Before Bo could continue, Henry interjected with some fatherly advice.

"Now, the best thing you can do, son, is not choose sides," Henry counseled. He reminded Bo that in conflicts between women, it was often best to remain neutral.

"You know, your mother and I separated for six months once," Henry shared, a mischievous glint in his eyes as he opened the grill to pour his secret barbecue sauce on the chicken.

Bo gasped in surprise. "Where did that come from, Dad? Wow!"

Henry slowly flipped the chicken pieces, chuckling as he took his time answering, letting the moment settle.

"I saw you did a little switch-a-roo of the subject talking about your sisters instead of your newly cut ex-wife."

The chilly breeze rustled through the nearby trees, mirroring the unexpected chill that had descended upon Bo.

Still baffled by the revelation, he asked, "Where is this story coming from?"

"It was around 1953, after a few years of marriage," Henry continued. He paused, his mind transporting him back in time.

Bo shifted his weight, the cold from the stone patio seeping into the soles of his shoes. The scent of hickory smoke wrapped around him, grounding him as his father's voice reached back across decades.

A letter had arrived unexpectedly from Henry's ex-girlfriend—who also happened to be his best friend's sister. She was asking for help. Her brother, Paul, was going through a deep depression. Barely eating, not leaving his room, unresponsive to her efforts. She wondered if Henry might visit. He hadn't seen Paul in years.

Lila was shaken. "Why are you acting like you're even considering this, Henry Ford Franklin?" She couldn't understand the loyalty Henry felt.

Back in high school, Paul and Henry were inseparable. One unforgettable moment that sealed their bond happened the year gangsters pressured them to throw a basketball game. Scared and outmatched, they agreed. Paul passed Henry the ball—he was supposed to miss. But the shot went in anyway. A complete accident... and a costly one.

The gangsters found them. But they had something crueler in mind than just revenge. They didn't beat Henry for making the shot. Instead, they made him watch. Held him back—helpless—as they pummeled Paul into the ground. That was their twisted punishment. Make the one who defied them live with the guilt. Make him carry it.

From that moment on, Henry and Paul were bound by more than friendship. It was trauma. Survival. A bond seared into their lives, deeper than blood. And now, all these years later, Paul needed him again.

Henry arranged a temporary transfer to Chicago through his job's distribution center. He didn't tell Lila the full story until the paperwork was finalized. When he finally did, her anger came like a storm—righteous, wounded, and sharp. She reminded him of their vows, of the life and responsibilities they had built together. But what cut deepest was the involvement of his ex-girlfriend. That part, she couldn't easily dismiss.

Still, Henry left.

When he arrived in Chicago, he was met not with temptation, but reality. Paul had suffered a devastating construction accident. He was confined to a wheelchair, struggling with depression, and barely eating. The ex-girlfriend? She was happily married, raising a child with her husband—a quiet man who welcomed Henry with unexpected grace and gratitude for coming to help.

Henry settled into a small apartment, juggling long work hours with caring for Paul. He wrote Lila every week, each letter a lifeline—sharing updates, describing the progress Paul was making, and expressing his longing to be home. He paid the bills for both households, rationed his phone calls due to the cost, and counted the days.

But weeks turned into months. Six of them.

When Henry finally returned home, the reunion was tense. Love was there, but it was buried under hurt and silence. It took the gentle guidance of their longtime pastor—and a series of raw, honest counseling sessions—for Henry and Lila to slowly rebuild. They unpacked years of assumptions, unspoken fears, and that painful season of absence. The counseling didn't fix things overnight, but it gave them language for their pain and a map toward reconciliation.

In time, something remarkable happened. Paul, along with his sister and her husband, relocated to their hometown for a fresh start. Henry had helped Paul get back on his feet, and the bond between them remained unshaken.

But the real surprise came in the quiet friendship that blossomed between Lila and Paul's sister—the very woman she had once resented. It didn't happen all at once. There were awkward hellos and cautious gatherings. But over time, through church events, shared meals, and moments of unexpected laughter, a sincere friendship grew. What began in jealousy and suspicion became something Lila never expected: trust.

Then, in 1956, Paul passed away unexpectedly. His death was a quiet blow to them all—a reminder of how fragile life was, and how sacred second chances could be.

The silence hung in the air. Bo stood still, smoke rising between them.

"Aunt Tracy..." he said slowly, disbelief tightening his voice. "You're telling me that Mom's best friend—the one who braided Selena and Lisa's hair every Saturday night before Sunday service, the one who brings the sweet potato pie no one dares compete with—that Aunt Tracy is your *ex*?"

Henry nodded, a knowing glint in his eye as he moved the meat from the grill into foil pans.

Bo gave a stunned chuckle, still trying to make sense of it. "Man... that's wild."

He squinted at the flames, the revelation branding itself into his memory like smoke into skin.

"Wow, Dad. You didn't have to share that with me... but thank you."

Henry looked up, his hands now still. "I told you because sometimes we want to rush to fix something that time still needs to work on. Your mama and I made it, but we had to go through it to grow through it. And it didn't happen overnight."

Bo nodded slowly, absorbing the weight of it.

"Sometimes time gives things back," Henry continued, "and sometimes it just gives you peace. Either way, if you let it—time will show you what's yours."

Bo looked out across the yard, the smoke thinning into the cold December air. His family might still be fractur ed... but maybe this wasn't the end.

Maybe time still had a surprise or two up its sleeve.

CHAPTER TEN

SAM & PAULA

REUNIONS & REVELATIONS

The crisp December air whipped at Sam's face as he pulled into the driveway, the familiar sight of his childhood home bringing a warmth that spread through his chest. He smiled, noticing his parents already had their famous blue lights on, even though it was still daylight. Before he could even put the car in park, the front door opened and his niece and nephew, Josh and Jordan, came bursting out.

"Uncle Sam! Aunt Paula!" Jordan rushed to give him a hug. "It's good to see you!"

She turned to her aunt, a hopeful look in her eyes, then grabbed Paula's hand and pulled her towards the house.

"Come on, Aunt Paula, we just baked cookies!"

Sam chuckled, watching them disappear inside with a stack of containers. He turned to Josh, who was already wrestling with the trunk, eager to help unload the mountain of gifts. Their family was still rather small—with his siblings, Bo and Selena, each having only one child, and Sam having twins—they always went all out with Christmas gifts.

"Whoa there, slow down!" Sam said. He grinned at Josh, who had shot up like a beanstalk since the last time he saw him. "Look at you, nephew! You must be about 6'3 now, right?"

Josh nodded, smiling with his mother's eyes. Sam couldn't help but instantly think about his ex-sister-in-law. He felt a pang of sympathy for her, and for his brother too. It had been a tough year for them all.

"How's your mom?" he asked, his genuine concern evident.

"She's doing fine," Josh replied, a hint of sadness in his voice. "Everybody here keeps asking about her."

"Well, she'll always be my sister-in-law," Sam reassured him.

"I thought Dad was handling everything well until we got here," Josh confided. "I overheard him telling Grandpa that he's going to get her back. That surprised me. Those two need to be friends."

Sam listened to Josh's insights, a frown creasing his forehead. He couldn't help but press further. "Come on, Josh, you know he still loves her. Don't you want to see them back together?"

Josh considered his words carefully, his love for his mother clear in his response. "It's not that, Uncle Sam," he explained. "My mom is so much happier now, not as grumpy as she used to be all the time. It's like she's a different person. It's good to see Mom happy."

"Well, you would know," Sam acknowledged. "You've had a front-row seat to it all. Sounds like your dad has a lot of work to do." He gave Josh another side hug as he sought to lighten the mood.

"Let's get the rest of these gifts in the house. You're going to love what we got you."

Sam watched his niece and nephew as they sorted through the names on the gifts, a smile tugging at his lips. He loved these chaotic gatherings, the laughter, the teasing, the way everyone seemed to pick up right where they left off. A Christmas carol played softly on the TV, as his mother loved the themed backgrounds on YouTube.

The aroma of freshly baked cookies called out to Sam as he reached for one on his mother's famous Santa Claus plate on the end table by the Christmas tree.

Since he and his siblings were kids, there was always something sweet and buttery on that plate.

Jordan, unable to contain her excitement, told them how she couldn't wait to reunite with her cousin Angela, whom she had missed dearly since the summer. Just as Jordan began to reminisce, Paula walked over from the corner where she had been on the phone.

A frown creased Paula's forehead as she shared Angela's update. Melissa—Angela's mentor and the wife of Bo's best friend—wouldn't be able to join them due to hospital visits. Dr. Darren would be accompanying Angela instead.

Sam couldn't conceal his surprise. *Darren was coming without his wife? On Christmas Eve?*

Darren, Bo's best friend since childhood and now a distinguished doctor, lived with his wife Melissa, a charge nurse, in San Diego—about 85 miles from Irvine and the surrounding areas where the Franklin family lived.

As a favor to his brother, Darren and Melissa had taken Angela under their wing, mentoring her as she adjusted to graduate school at Loma Linda School of Medicine and life away from home.

Before anyone could comment, the front door swung open with a bang. Angel, Angela's twin brother, burst in, full of lively energy, a playful sparkle in his eyes.

Sam felt a comforting warmth spread through him as he hugged his son. A strong scent of cedar wood filled the air around them and Angel's fitted muscle shirt strained against his broad shoulders, making his strong build look even more impressive. But Sam was thrown off by Paula's cold and clammy touch on his arm as her face flushed with embarrassment at their son's appearance.

"Merry Christmas everybody!" Angel shouted, as he hurried to drop something off before visiting his girl-friend.

"Hey, son. Did you go to your girlfriend's house already?" Paula asked.

"I'm on my way to Vivica's house now," Angel replied.

"What a tight shirt, you look like you're ready for the Chippendales show in Vegas," Paula remarked, her words laced with sarcasm.

Josh and Jordan chuckled as they admired their cousin and greeted him with glee. Sam, however, immediately tried to catch Paula's eye, hoping she remembered the chat they'd just had on the drive over. But he could tell she intentionally ignored him.

Undeterred, Angel thankfully flashed a self-assured smile. "You have to admit, Mom, I look good."

But Paula was quick to voice her concerns. "You don't want to embarrass us, especially at Vivica's parents' house. Where are your Christmas pajamas, like all of us?"

Angel defended his choice, asserting his adulthood. "Mom, I can't go to her parents' house in my pajamas."

Sam nodded in approval, giving his son a fist bump. He respected that his son didn't want to show up at his girlfriend's house in pajamas. However, he knew the look of annoyance in his son's eyes and braced himself for the rebuttal.

"I bet if it was Angela, it would be just fine," Angel remarked.

Paula wasn't swayed. "Angela doesn't have a boyfriend."

Angel smirked. "You don't know everything about Angela."

Paula maintained her ground. "Angela tells me everything."

Angel persisted. "That's what you think, Mom. Why can't I get the same love Angela gets?"

The warmth in the room vanished as Josh and Jordan gave each other nervous looks. Sensing the tension, they quickly made their exit.

Watching the kids instinctively leave the room, their faces etched with anticipation, Sam felt a surge of protectiveness. He had to put a stop to this. His wife and his son were matching each other's energy, and it was creating a ripple effect through the whole room.

"Come on now, it's Christmas Eve," Sam interjected, his voice firm. He caught Paula's eye this time, silently urging her to ease up. Just as he was putting the fire out, his father Henry made his entrance carrying a pan of steaming barbecue chicken legs.

"Hey there. I thought I heard more voices. I have about an hour left on the grill before we eat," Henry announced. He quickly covered the pan with foil, set it on the counter, and returned to the living room to embrace his family.

The humorous atmosphere continued as Henry couldn't resist making a playful remark about Angel's attire.

"What in the gynecologist do you have on, Angel?"

Angel, with a lighthearted spirit, decided to engage in the banter. "Gynecologist? Men don't go to the gynecologist, Pops."

"I know, but your girlfriend is going to have to see one if you keep wearing stuff like that," Henry countered with a mischievous glint in his eye, giving his son Sam a high-five.

A chorus of laughter filled the room as Angel played along. "Aww, Pops, you got jokes."

Sam was happy to see his son accept the jest with a smile. As Angel took his leave, Paula couldn't help but express her concern, calling after him.

"Angel, Angel."

As Angel left, Sam stepped in, holding his wife intimately by the waist. "It'll be alright, Paula," he assured her gently.

But Paula, exasperated by her son's fashion choices and perhaps a multitude of other concerns, couldn't help but let her frustration show. "Lord, that boy," she muttered.

Lighting the mood, Henry interjected, "You keep holding your wife like that, she'll be needing a gynecologist too!"

His father's playful grin and well-timed joke sparked another round of laughter, his knack for light-hearted teasing always bringing the room to life.

As Henry invited everyone to explore his new grill, Sam kissed Paula with reassurance as they headed to the backyard. Although inside, between the news of her wanting to go off on her own for New Year's Eve and her hostile behavior towards their son, he was sure she was having a mid-life crisis.

CHAPTER ELEVEN

LISA

BONDS & BOUNDARIES

Lisa parked down the street, the neighborhood already crowded with cars as families gathered for the holiday. As she stepped out and closed the door behind her, she paused—just for a moment—to take it all in. Home was only a few houses away, but the feeling had already arrived.

Bo was already jogging toward her, his breath puffing in the cold. "Need help?" he called out.

"Always," she joked, popping open the trunk. Her hand brushed against a glittery gift bag, and she winced as the corner poked her wrist. "Ouch. That little sucker hurt."

With a laugh, Bo lifted the bigger boxes, and together they walked toward the front porch. Lisa noticed the porch light was still glowing and shook her head. Her parents never remembered to switch it off. She twisted the door handle—unlocked, as usual—and rolled her eyes affectionately.

"They never lock this door," she muttered.

Bo chuckled, setting down the gifts on the living room couch. "Look at you, little sis, with all the holiday spirit," he teased, eyeing her bright red pajama set.

Lisa flicked one of the fluffy fur cuffs at her wrist. "You know me—I like a little extra pizzazz," she said, feeling the soft faux fur brush against her palm.

"Is the extra pizzazz because of a new boyfriend?"

Bo's teasing about her love life made her shrug it off with a casual laugh. She tried to keep it light, though her heart fluttered with unspoken emotions she wasn't ready to share.

"You're so nosy, Bo," Lisa said, half-joking. But she saw the concern in his eyes—he sensed more than she wanted to reveal.

He set down the rest of the boxes and studied her for a moment. "No, really. Are you good?" he asked, quietly.

"Now that I'm divorced, I get the loneliness."

Lisa's chest tightened. Hearing Bo admit his own struggles reminded her how new this was for him—his first Christmas without Trinity. She thought of her own divorce a few years back and how raw it had left her.

"This is your first Christmas party without Trinity," she said gently.

She opened her arms, and Bo stepped into her embrace. The feel of his jacket pressing against her cheek, the familiar warmth of a sibling's hug, grounded her. She remembered the heartache, the uncertainty—and how it helped to have family close.

"I know what it's like," she whispered, rubbing gentle circles on his back. "How's Chachi?" she asked, a playful smile tugging at her lips.

Bo snorted, shaking his head. "Josh is fifteen now, and you know he hates that nickname."

Lisa laughed under her breath. "He'll always be Chachi to me. How's he doing with you and Trinity?"

"He's been a huge help, actually." Bo shifted, lifting his shoulders. "By the way... Selena is here," he added, almost offhand, but Lisa noticed the slight pause before he said her name. Her whole body tensed. It was like her mind replayed every tense conversation they'd ever had.

"I saw her car outside," Lisa said, keeping her tone clipped. Selena's fondness for Lisa's ex-husband had driven a wedge between them, and she still hadn't shaken off Selena's constant judgment.

Right on cue, Selena strolled into the living room, a pair of oversized sunglasses perched on her nose. It felt dramatic, and Lisa couldn't help an inward eye-roll.

"Hey, guys," Selena greeted with a casual wave.

Bo, ever the peacekeeper, nervously gave her another hug. "What's up, big sis?"

The air instantly thickened. Selena's wave made it clear she wasn't interested in a hug. Feeling petty, Lisa's gaze flicked over the sunglasses as she offered a half-hearted wave.

"Since when do we wear shades inside?" she teased, trying to keep the jab light but unable to hide her irritation.

"It's Christmas, guys. Please don't start," Bo pleaded, encouraging a friendlier exchange.

Just then, Lisa's phone buzzed—a small mercy.

"I'd better take this," she muttered, stepping into the hallway. She heard Selena mumble something under her breath—maybe about her—but let it go.

Inside the sewing room, she checked her screen. Spam call. Of course. Still, she lingered, pressing her free hand against the old wooden sewing table and exhaling the tension Selena always stirred.

The door swung open. Paula entered, startling her. "Hey, sister-in-law! Look at these cute pajamas. Did they come with the fur, or did you add that?"

Grateful for the distraction, Lisa leaned into Paula's warm hug. "I added it myself," she said, flicking one of the fluffy cuffs. "Gotta have my flair."

Lowering her voice with a mock-serious tone, she added, "I just ran into your 'ugly' sister-in-law in the living room."

Paula snorted with laughter. "So, you two are still not speaking?"

Lisa shrugged, the old heaviness returning. "I don't know, Paula. My sister has never liked me. Or at least, that's how it feels."

"You know that's not true," Paula said gently. "You two need to kiss and make up."

Lisa rolled her eyes. "She looks ridiculous wearing sunglasses in the house."

"She said she had a headache," Paula replied, waving off the complaint with a smile. "The lights were bothering her. Go easy on her, okay? How've you been?"

"I'm doing pretty good," Lisa said—and then smiled wider. "Actually, really good."

She grabbed Paula's hand. "Come here." She pulled her into the sewing room and shut the door. On her phone, she brought up a photo of an extravagant floral arrangement: "Please go out with me" spelled out in blossoms.

Lisa smiled shyly. "It's from Liam Grayson."

Paula gasped. "Liam Grayson? That man is gorgeous. You better say yes!"

Lisa blushed. She fiddled with the fur trim of her sleeve. "I told myself I'd never date another pro athlete."

Paula raised a brow. "Maybe just enjoy the moment. No one's asking you to marry him."

Lisa smiled at the screen, the flowers triggering a flutter in her stomach. Paula stood beside her, practically buzzing. "He's got style," she teased. "Flowers that spell a message? Come on!"

Just then, Lisa's phone rang. Liam's name lit up the screen.

"Oh my gosh, answer it!" Paula mouthed, fanning herself.

Lisa swiped to accept, steadying her breath. "Hello?"

"Hey, Lisa," Liam said, his voice warm and easy. "Just checking if you got the flowers—and to make sure you weren't allergic."

Lisa grinned. "All good on the allergy front." She turned away, but Paula leaned closer, one hand to her ear, listening in.

Paula bounced silently. "He's so sweet!"

"Thanks for thinking of me," Lisa said. "They're... beautiful." Paula leaned dramatically against the sewing table, fanning herself with a grin.

"Anything for you," Liam said. "I won't keep you—just wanted to say Merry Christmas and... I'd love to see you soon if you're free."

Lisa's heart skipped. "Let's talk after the holidays," she said, trying to sound calm.

"Sounds good. Enjoy your family."

When the call ended, Lisa let out a long breath.

"He is so into you!" Paula squealed.

Lisa laughed. "You're team too much."

"One date won't kill you," Paula said. "If those flowers are any sign, you might have a keeper."

Lisa's heart fluttered again. Maybe this could be something special. For the first time in a long time, she felt hope.

"I guess I could just go on one date," she said softly.

"There you go." Paula grinned. "No harm in enjoying a good meal."

Lisa smiled, a spark of anticipation shimmering inside. "Yeah," she admitted. "I guess I am curious about him."

"Ooh, I bet he smells amazing," Paula teased.

They both laughed, the sound echoing like teenage girls gushing over a crush. For a moment, Lisa forgot the tension with Selena.

In that quiet joy, she realized: maybe this Christmas could hold more than past regrets. Maybe something new was just beginning.

Chapter Twelve

SELENA & LISA

Unshared Lives

S elena pressed a stack of freshly laundered linens against her hip, her gaze drifting down the hallway. She paused as she caught a glimpse of Lisa and Paula passing by, laughing, just as she closed the closet door. From where she stood, they looked like teenagers sharing secrets—heads bent close, giggles echoing off the walls.

A twinge of envy tugged at Selena's chest. She'd never developed that kind of easy camaraderie with her sister-in-law—or, if she was being honest, with Lisa. Watching them now, she wondered if things might have been different if she'd let herself be more open. But she quickly pushed the thought aside. There was a dining room table to set, and she wasn't about to get sentimental over a bonding moment that clearly didn't include her.

She carried the linens toward the dining room, her footsteps muffled by the thick carpet. Setting them down, she scanned the half-set table: mismatched silverware Bo must have pulled from the drawer, a few unevenly spaced plates, and a folded stack of napkins. "No one can do anything properly around here," she muttered, carefully smoothing the tablecloth.

As she straightened the napkins, her gaze caught the family photos on the wall. A reunion snapshot with Lisa front and center, beaming. One of Bo and Lisa in Little League uniforms. And off to the side, a faded photo of her teenage self, stiff in a modest skirt, trying too hard to appear composed. A pang of regret struck her. *I was just a kid*, she thought. *But I never really got to be one.*

Her mother had poured responsibility onto her shoulders early. With both parents working, Selena had become the default caregiver—cooking, cleaning, ironing, and keeping the house in order. There had been no slumber parties, no carefree afternoons. Just lists of chores and expectations.

She tugged at the hem of her sweater, agitated by the stark contrast between the few posed photos of her and the carefree candids of Bo and Lisa. She'd brought it up once, only for her mother to dismiss her. *"You're too old to feel any type of way,"* she'd said. After all, Bo and Lisa were still kids when Selena had already moved out.

Another burst of laughter rang out from the hallway. Lisa and Paula again. The pang returned—regret, resentment, something unspoken. *If I'd tried harder, would I have had a bond like that too?*

Her phone chimed, pulling her out of thought. A message from her husband, the beginning of his usual apology tour. She inhaled deeply and exhaled slow, placing the final mat under a plate.

There's no time to dwell on old wounds, she reminded herself. *Not when I've got real problems now.* But the bitterness clung to her ribs like something long-settled and hard to shake. She couldn't help but feel cheated—like Lisa had been handed a life she never had the chance to imagine.

She remembered the day their mother announced she was pregnant again. Selena had sat at the kitchen table, legs swinging, quietly chanting in her head: *Not a girl. Please not a girl.* But of course, it was.

By the time Lisa was old enough for teenage freedoms, the religious rules had softened. While Selena had been scolded for even asking to see a movie, Lisa had glittery manicures, open-toed shoes, and a custom prom dress sewn by their mother.

Over time, resentment grew, even if she never said it aloud. Lisa had received freedom, approval, and indulgence. Not intentionally—but still. It was hard to ignore.

She thought of a moment long ago: Lisa, wide-eyed, asking for help after getting her period. Selena had brushed her off with a clipped, "Now you can get pregnant." Not to be cruel. She just hadn't known what else to say. *Maybe I should've been there for her,* Selena thought, wiping an invisible smudge from a picture frame. *But I was trying to survive too.*

Selena had married quickly, eager to escape the rules. She built a life that looked freer on the outside—successful husband, one child, fewer restrictions. But the guardedness she'd learned at home followed her into that life too. Old habits.

What stung most now was Lisa's ease—her career in sports journalism, her access to opportunities, the way men seemed to respect her. Lisa drove a brand-new car. Selena's first was a rusty hand-me-down.

It's not that I wanted her to suffer. But still—it felt unjust.

She sighed and pressed her thumb along the edge of a picture. She knew the resentment wasn't fair. But fairness had always felt out of reach.

***

From the kitchen, Lisa watched her sister from a distance. Selena seemed lost in thought as she set the table, unaware that anyone was watching. Lisa smirked slightly. Maybe it was those ridiculous sunglasses she insisted on wearing indoors.

She ran her fingertips over the edge of an old plate, one her mother had asked her to retrieve for the cookie bars. A hairline crack ran through it—one Lisa had glued years ago. She always thought it was beautiful in a broken sort of way.

Just like her bond with Selena. She'd been trying to "glue" them together her whole life. But some pieces don't fit no matter how carefully you arrange them.

As a child, Lisa had idolized her older sister. She had craved her approval, her advice, her attention. But every time she asked a question—about boys, about clothes, about growing up—Selena brushed her off.

Their mother, Lila, spoke in soft warnings and vague life lessons. She avoided uncomfortable topics, which left Lisa grasping for truth in a house full of quiet judgment.

She remembered getting her period in sixth grade. She'd gone straight to Selena, hoping for a sisterly moment. Selena's only response was, "Now you can get pregnant." That was it. No warmth. No comfort. Just a line passed down like a baton. Lisa didn't blame her—at least not entirely. That's just how it was in their house. But still, it hurt.

Even now, as a grown woman with a career and independence, Lisa still longed for her sister's approval. And she never quite got it. She sometimes wondered if Selena saw her as spoiled. The car at sixteen. The custom dress. The newer, gentler rules. It wasn't her fault the family had changed. She hadn't asked for any of it.

Still, the invisible wall remained. No matter how many times she tried to reach across it, Selena stayed closed off. Lisa had long since stopped trying to decode her. She found it easier to confide in her male colleagues—at least they said what they meant.

Now, watching Selena from the kitchen, Lisa couldn't help but feel a little sorry. Maybe it wasn't just resentment. Maybe it was pain, too.

Her thoughts broke when her mother handed her the tray of cookie bars. Lisa began placing them on the serving plate, fingers pausing briefly at the spot where the plate had been glued. Selena probably thinks I had it easy, Lisa thought. And maybe I did. But it wasn't perfect.

She placed the last bar down, her heart caught between memory and hope. *Maybe one day we'll talk. Really talk.*

Until then, they remained two women raised by the same hands, shaped by different decades, still circling the same dining room—bound by blood, but separated by silence.

Chapter Thirteen

ANGELA

Beneath The Surface

Angela pulled up to the curb, eyes settling on the row of cars already crowded into her grandparents' driveway. Recognizing her parents' SUV and her aunt's sedan confirmed she and Darren were the last to arrive.

A flutter of nerves tightened in her chest, and she drummed her fingers on the steering wheel to steady the jittery feeling in her stomach. Beside her, Darren unbuckled his seatbelt and glanced her way.

"You all right? You seem a little tense."

"I'm fine," Angela replied, though her shoulders felt tight. "Just... everyone's probably inside waiting, and there's always a million questions about med school.

And my parents—" She stopped, realizing she was rambling.

"You'll do great," Darren assured, offering a comforting smile. "I'm here with you."

With a deep breath, Angela switched off the ignition. She stepped out into the mild afternoon air, feeling a cold breeze brush across her cheeks. From the backyard came the buzz of conversation, and she smiled as the familiar blue glow of lights danced across the front of her grandparents' home.

"Hey, we made it," she said as they stepped into the house. She ran a hand through her hair, hoping she looked at least somewhat composed.

Darren nodded, observing the Christmas decor of the living room he was familiar with. "Nice. I see your grandparents are still leaving the door open."

Angela chuckled, exhaling some of her nerves. "They sure do. The whole neighborhood does that."

Darren grinned. "Old school."

"You know I love the old school," Angela confessed, a twinkle in her eyes. A flush of warmth rose in her chest, the comfort of being back at her grandparents' home mixing with a subtle excitement she couldn't quite name.

She let her gaze drift across the living room—a set of mahogany chairs paired with a coffee table, where a bright poinsettia arrangement took center stage—before it settled on her favorite family photo propped on the mantel. It was an old picture of her grandmother wearing her signature smile, and Angela felt a small wave of calm settle over her.

"Man, I hope Melissa can still come," Darren remarked, looking around with anticipation as he followed Angela into the living room.

"I know. Well, I guess it's just me and you," Angela said, her voice softening. "Oh, remember you have to take your medicine at three," she offered as a gentle reminder. "You want me to remind you?" She glanced at her phone's clock, the quiet hum of the air conditioner clicking on in the background.

Darren smiled warmly, appreciating her thoughtfulness. "I got it."

Their hands accidentally brushed against each other. Angela felt a light, pleasant tingle at the brief contact, her pulse fluttering.

"We need to catch a movie while we're here."

Darren eagerly agreed. "Cool. Is everybody going?"

Angela, ever the conscientious one, added, "Oh yeah, of course. Did you remember to turn the lights off?"

Darren realized he had forgotten and reached for his phone. "Let me check. You're right, I forgot. Let me turn them off. Good looking out, Angel."

The slow burn of her grandmother's candle on the table scented the air, causing Angela to sneeze.

"God bless you."

Unbeknownst to them, Mayreen, Angela's play cousin, hidden from view, was observing their interaction from a chair in the corner of the room.

"Well, aren't you Ms. Thoughtful?" Mayreen playfully interjected, with a smug look on her face.

Startled, Angela and Darren turned to find Mayreen standing before them with a suspicious look. With cheeks flushed, Angela introduced her cousin to Darren.

"Oh hey, girl. We didn't see you. This is Dr. Darren. You know, Uncle Bo's friend—my mentor."

Mayreen, with a curious tilt of her head, couldn't help but point out, "Why are you calling her 'Angel'?"

Darren, always quick on his feet, chimed in with a chuckle, "Oh, it's just a nickname. Nice to meet you."

Mayreen nodded. "That's her brother's name," she said sarcastically.

Angela quickly interjected, "Oh yes, I can't wait to see Angel."

Mayreen's presence had already added a touch of tension, but her keen eye quickly noticed something different about her cousin.

Angela was more dressed up than usual—a subtle transformation that didn't escape Mayreen's discerning gaze. She couldn't help but exclaim, "Angela, you're looking all fancy today. I've never known you to really wear makeup."

Angela's cheeks flushed with embarrassment, especially in front of Darren. She brushed a stray lock of hair behind her ear and replied somewhat defensively, "Oh, well, I just thought... you know, it's a family gathering."

She could feel the messy assumption behind Mayreen's gaze, her palms lightly sweating in self-consciousness.

Darren, ever the gentleman, interjected with a compliment. "You look great, Angela."

Mayreen raised an eyebrow and leaned in, her eyes lingering on Angela's polished appearance. "Any reason for the change?"

Angela smiled sheepishly and confessed, "I guess you're right. I'm usually knee-deep in books and don't have time to get dolled up."

Mayreen wasn't finished inspecting her cousin's transformation and noticed Angela's well-manicured nails. "Since when does a med student have a full set of nails?"

Angela's embarrassment deepened, and she hurried to clarify, "Well, I'm not a doctor yet."

"You look all dolled up for a date." Satisfied with her interjection, Mayreen gave Angela a pointed look. "We need to talk," she said before leaving Angela and Darren alone once more.

Recovering from the unexpected encounter, Darren expressed his amazement. "That was crazy."

Angela, still slightly taken aback, rolled her eyes. "My cousin is too messy. Anyway, I really hope Melissa can catch a flight out."

As their eyes locked, a faint burst of laughter could be heard in the backyard, reminding Angela that more family awaited. The tantalizing scent of barbecue wafted through the air.

"Something is smelling good," Darren noted with appreciation.

"That's Pops' barbecue. Let's go. Everybody will be happy to see you—especially Uncle Bo."

As they headed out to the backyard, Angela felt a whirlwind of thoughts racing through her mind. She had excelled in her academic pursuits, earning her place in medical school, but with every achievement came an added layer of pressure to meet the bar that had been set so high.

The demands of medical school were unforgiving, and Angela had been forced to make tough decisions. She transitioned from full-time work to a part-time job to accommodate her grueling schedule—a move necessary to navigate the complexities of her studies.

However, there was one secret Angela had kept from her parents. She hadn't mentioned that she'd lost her apartment—a situation that caught her off guard after reducing her work hours.

It had happened while her parents were away on an extended trip, and rather than burden them with stress from afar, Angela decided to handle it on her own. She turned to the one person she trusted most—her Uncle Bo. He was the only family member she confided in, and it was his idea that led Darren and Melissa to open their home and hearts to her for a temporary stay.

Angela had given her parents the impression that she was just spending a few nights at her mentors' home to study for important exams. She planned to move into a new place by summer and assumed they'd never need to know the full truth. Bo, unaware that Sam and Paula weren't in the loop, believed they already knew.

Darren, a seasoned physician on sabbatical, was often at home, and his wife, Melissa, a dedicated nurse, was typically at work. These circumstances had allowed Angela and Darren to grow closer, bonding over her aspirations to become a doctor.

It was Darren's presence at home that began to reveal the subtle shift in Angela's feelings. She found herself admiring Darren not only for his expertise but also for the kindness he extended to her. As days turned into weeks, and weeks into months, Angela and Darren found themselves slowly drawn to each other.

Although their feelings remained in check, their connection was developing into a melody of unvoiced emotions that danced beneath the surface. As they ventured into the heart of the family gathering, greeting everyone, the secret connection between Angela and Darren remained hidden in the shadows—awaiting the day when it would be whispered into the light.

CHAPTER FOURTEEN

LILA & SAM

THE SANCTUARY WITHIN

As Lila stood on the balcony, the warmth of her favorite coffee cup cradled in her hands, she embraced the fleeting moment of solitude. The cool breeze caressed her face, carrying the weight of her unspoken prayers. Her gaze drifted over the softly glowing Christmas lights shining in the distance before lifting to the endless sky.

She had slipped away for a brief moment while the family gathered downstairs, craving time alone with God and the hushed whispers of her heart. The situation with Selena weighed heavily on her mind, and she silently petitioned for peace in the storm that brewed.

The worry lines etched on her forehead mirrored the tumultuous currents beneath her surface composure.

Nervousness lingered as she wondered what might happen if her husband and sons found out what Richard had done.

As if on cue, the door creaked open, and her eldest son, Sam, entered the room, his eyes reflecting concern and curiosity.

"There you are, Mom," he greeted, his voice a gentle interruption to the silent symphony of Lila's thoughts. "I was wondering where you went."

"I was wondering when you would join me," Lila said, a wistful smile playing on her lips.

Sam, taken aback by her revelation, inquired about the meaning behind her words.

"I could see it all in your wife's face. Every woman needs something that is just hers." She watched Sam settle into the chair beside her on the balcony, adjusting his seat nervously as a mix of surprise danced in his eyes.

Lila, sensing the unspoken weight on her son's shoulders, invited him to share his thoughts. "What's on your mind, son?"

Sam hesitated, his gaze lingering over his parents' panoramic view of the mountains before he finally unraveled the inner turmoil weighing on his mind.

"Paula wants to discover herself without me, and I don't quite know how to take that," he confessed, his words uncertain and vulnerable.

"When we go on vacations together, sometimes we separate and do our own things, and that's fine. At the end of the day, we always come back together and discuss our adventures. But now Paula wants to go on a trip for a few days by herself. She says nothing is wrong, but I don't like it."

Lila, with a knowing gaze, took a moment before responding, quietly observing the concern etched on her son's face.

A thin strand of hair escaped her updo, brushing against her cheek in the breeze. Taking another sip of her coffee, she let the warmth center her own thoughts. Her mind traveled back to the pages of her own life's narrative as she began to recount the memories.

"Let me tell you a little story."

For two days out of every month, Henry escaped his daily life of work and family into the solitude of nature, where the only sounds were the rustling leaves and the gentle lapping of water against his rented boat.

As Lila recounted the story, the balcony became a portal to the past, a place where the echoes of laughter and closeness lingered in the air.

These trips were more than just fishing expeditions; they were a sanctuary for Henry and his best friend Carl to reflect on their lives, dreams, and, most importantly, their friendship.

Carl once told her that those trips allowed them to rediscover themselves, away from the roles of husbands and fathers. It was a sacred time when they could be just Henry and Carl, two friends navigating the currents of life.

Lila continued, the memories unfolding like pages from one of her well-worn journals. Her gaze fixed on a swaying palm tree beyond the balcony railing.

In the beginning, Lila wasn't too fond of Carl, but he grew on her with his infectious laughter and support of Henry. Lila accepted their friendship as a pact between brothers.

"When Henry would embark on those trips, I stopped merely waiting for his return; I embraced the solitude as an opportunity for self-discovery myself," Lila explained.

Extended visits with her parents and sisters became a source of comfort, a reminder that love existed beyond the confines of her marriage. Those days spent with her family allowed her to strengthen the ties that grounded her.

Lila's gaze turned inward as she gently swirled the cup in her hand to even the warmth, retracing the steps of her past.

There were also times during Henry's fishing trips when she craved solitude. She'd escape to her favorite department store or take time to read her favorite books. She reveled in those moments. It wasn't about detachment; it was about carving out a space for individual growth within the shared expanse of marriage.

And then, unexpectedly, Carl passed away, and Henry was engulfed in a storm of grief that took a toll on him. In his despair, he inadvertently took his anger out on Lila.

Every suppressed emotion, every unspoken word, erupted like a dormant volcano. The pain of loss became a tempest, and Lila, standing in its path, felt the brunt of its fury. The vulnerability in Lila's voice was surprising even to herself as she observed the expression on Sam's face as he listened.

One day, as Henry reminisced about the fishing lodge, Lila noticed a flicker of light in his eyes—a nostalgic glow in the shadows of grief. He spoke of the brotherhood with Carl and the other fishing buddies, sharing the laughter and stories from the bond forged on the banks of those waters.

"I began to understand the depth of his connection to those memories, the way they anchored him to a time of joy with his friends. Then one day it dawned on me," Lila continued, her eyes reflecting the narrative in her heart.

Lila proposed that Henry return to the fishing lodge, where he could connect and confront the absence of Carl. Henry hesitated; the prospect of revisiting that sacred space without his dear friend caused ripples of uncertainty. But Lila, hopeful, encouraged him to take that first step toward healing.

Henry found the courage to revisit the hallowed grounds of the fishing lodge, but instead of the usual two-day adventure with Carl, he decided on a different path—a half-day excursion.

And in a twist of fate, Henry encountered an old acquaintance at the lodge—a serendipitous reunion that breathed life back into his soul. "Your father shared the news of Carl's passing, and in the spirit of kindness, the man asked your dad to join him and his partners."

Shared laughter and stories rekindled the spirit of brotherhood, and Henry was able to find peace. That acquaintance became a friend, and Henry joined several future excursions.

Placing Sam's hand in hers, Lila turned to him and said, "And that, my dear Sam, is the serendipitous genesis of the family friend you affectionately call Uncle Lewis."

Taken aback by the backstory of his father and Uncle Lewis, Sam couldn't help but express a gentle lament to his mother. "You know, Mom," Sam began, his voice touched with awe, "these are stories we should know. Why hadn't you ever shared them with us?"

Lila's eyes, carrying the weight of a bygone era, responded with a sigh. "I don't know," she admitted, melancholy woven into her words.

"My parents never really shared stories of their past with us, and neither did Henry's. When we were raised, you just didn't talk about things."

Realizing that this shared history helped her son, Lila's maternal gaze offered a tender smile.

"Sharing our personal stories is not the norm for my generation, besides little nuggets of wisdom, but maybe it's time to change that."

With quiet assurance, Lila suggested to Sam that Paula was not abandoning the sanctuary of their marriage; rather, she was in the pursuit of balance. The canvas of Paula's identity in the roles of mother and wife was now unfolding into new chapters. Lila gently continued, her words a soothing balm to Sam.

"It's an opportunity for both of you to rediscover something new about yourselves." She encouraged Sam to let this be a chapter of exploration, not a page of apprehension. The symphony of a lasting marriage often incorporates solo movements, where each partner finds harmony within themselves.

Lila watched as Sam rose from his chair, a sense of newfound clarity permeating the air. He embraced his mother, enveloping her in a hug reminiscent of their moments together when he was a child.

Closing her eyes, Lila absorbed the love as she hugged her son tight. Sam vowed to nurture his marriage and prioritize his wife's needs, telling Lila he recognized the sacrifices she had made for their family.

He understood the importance of allowing Paula to explore her own desires and passions. He shared with Lila his love for photography and how he would really like to start exploring it more—and would even love to take a few classes, maybe even go on a few excursions himself.

As Sam left, Lila smiled and looked up to the sky. Her thoughts drifted to each of her children: Sam, who now carried a new resolve; Selena, whose silent struggles weighed heavily on her heart; Bo, adjusting to his recent divorce; and Lisa, who was surprisingly happy.

She cherished being a mother, especially during the Christmas season when unity and tradition felt more precious than ever. The memories of Christmases past—early-morning giggles, flour-dusted countertops, and torn wrapping paper strewn about the living room—flickered in her mind's eye. She took the final sip of her coffee, savoring its warmth before setting the cup aside.

From downstairs, the distant hum of laughter and the faint clatter of dishes beckoned her back to the family gathering. With a soft sigh, she stepped inside, letting the rich aroma of cinnamon and freshly baked pies guide her toward the kitchen.

Chapter Fifteen

LISA, PAULA, & SELENA

BEHIND CLOSED DOORS

As Bo's departing footsteps faded down the hall, Lisa's conversation with Paula slowed to an awkward stop. She'd been half-listening to her sister-in-law's chatter when she noticed Selena hovering in the doorway of the sewing room. A familiar prickle of unease tightened in Lisa's chest—Selena rarely hesitated unless she wanted something.

"Let me go check on Mom," Lisa announced, pushing off the small couch. She wanted an excuse to duck out before the tension escalated.

Paula shot her a disapproving glance. "Come on, Lisa," she said quietly. "Let's act our age."

Lisa paused, feeling the air thicken. She'd grown used to how Selena could toss subtle digs like little darts. Over the years, Selena had turned it into an art form, and now Lisa braced herself for the usual cutting comments. But there was something hesitant in Selena's posture that set Lisa even more on edge.

Lisa's patience wore thin as Paula stubbornly blocked her attempts to leave. A knot of tension formed in her stomach the moment her sister entered the sewing room, and she felt a strong urge to get out of there.

Then, something shifted inside her when she really took in Selena's appearance. She was surprisingly disheveled—so unlike her usual proper self, always reminding everyone of her doctorate. A sudden spark of boldness flared in Lisa when her gaze landed on her sister's dark sunglasses, worn indoors.

"Wow, it sure is sunny in here. Nice sunglasses," she said, her voice laced with quiet sarcasm.

The words dripped with passive aggression. Lisa would take charge of this uneasy standoff rather than sit back and wait for Selena to lash out first. As soon as the jab escaped her lips, a little rush of adrenaline zinged through her—a small victory in a room thick with unspoken tension. A smirk tugged at her mouth.

But Selena, who could usually cut down a room with a single glance, suddenly faltered. Her voice caught in her throat, and tears spilled down her cheeks, shocking Lisa and Paula into silence.

No retort. Only tears.

Lisa's breath hitched. For a moment, she couldn't quite process what she was seeing. Selena's shoulders shook with quiet sobs, and the tears carved streaks through the powder on her face.

The shield of sunglasses slipped a bit, revealing a swollen eye that looked desperately vulnerable—a sight Lisa had never expected to see in her razor-tongued sister.

Their interaction often a stage for sarcastic exchange, hushed under Selena's unexpected breakdown. Lisa glanced at Paula, uncertain how to react. Part of her felt a guilty pang for delivering that jab, but another part of her was stunned by this raw display.

She'd never seen Selena like this—never imagined she could break in front of them. And though the tension remained, compassion and alarm tugged at Lisa's chest.

With a deliberate slowness, Selena lowered her sunglasses all the way, unveiling a stark, pink bruise beneath.

The sight of the blackened eye left Lisa and Paula in a state of utter shock—Lisa's gasp escaped her throat, echoing through the room. Despite the distant relationship she'd maintained with her sister, Lisa felt a fierce protective instinct surge to the forefront.

"What happened?" she asked, her voice soft but urgent, a genuine concern shaking loose all the old resentments.

The revelation of Selena's injury tore through the barriers of their strained interactions, replacing tension with worry for her well-being. The silence felt so thick, Lisa could almost taste it as they waited for Selena's explanation.

Selena recounted the argument that had spiraled into chaos over the family Christmas gifts, her tone faltering every so often as she divulged the shocking truth: Richard had hit her because of it.

Appalled by the revelation, Lisa and Paula rushed to Selena's side, exchanging a stunned glance. Their initial confusion gave way to an eruption of emotions—anger, concern, and an overwhelming desire to protect Selena.

"Where is Richard?" Lisa's voice cracked, the mere mention of his name triggering a knot of rage in her stomach. She clenched her jaw, feeling the weight of the moment press heavily on her heart.

"No, no, no." Selena implored with desperation, her voice trembling. "Please, stop, Lisa. What do you know about marriage?"

Lisa cringed, the unexpected retort striking like a slap to the face. "You're sitting there with a black eye and taking a shot at me?" she spat out instantly, her tone filled with disgust and hurt.

The accusation dug deep, hitting a nerve. Paula, attempting to diffuse the escalating, interjected with urgency. "Please, guys, this is serious," she pleaded, her gaze darting between them.

From Lisa's vantage point, Selena's earlier tears seemed distant, replaced by this sudden hostility. Yet the words hung heavily in the air as if Selena realized too late she'd crossed a line.

"I'm sorry, Lisa," she murmured, her voice hushed and remorseful. "I shouldn't have said that."

Lisa blinked, still stung. Over the years, Selena had been known to toss out insincere apologies, but this time, there was an earnestness that struck a chord. "Really, Lisa, I'm sorry." It was a rare moment of vulnerability—a crack Lisa hadn't often seen in her sister's guarded exterior.

"I just can't believe Richard put me in this kind of situation. What if Dad and the guys find out?" Selena asked, her voice trembling slightly.

Lisa felt a quick stab of empathy for her sister's predicament. It would be disastrous if her Dad and brothers found out. The way Selena reacted hurt but she decided to let it go. She watched Selena's shoulders tense as she began describing the frantic moments before leaving the house.

"I just took off with Jordan before things could escalate."

From the pinched look in Selena's eyes, Lisa sensed she was replaying every chaotic second. Paula, her concern obvious in the tight set of her jaw, probed further. "Did Jordan witness any of it?" she asked, her worried gaze darting between Selena and Lisa.

"No, thank God." Selena exhaled, sounding momentarily relieved. "But she did hear everything."

Selena paused, her hand hovering as if she couldn't decide where to place it. Then, she finally admitted the conversation she'd had with Jordan, halting slightly on each word, as though unsure how much to reveal.

"I finally told Jordan everything, and she doesn't want to go home." Selena continued, her voice quivering as she recounted the unexpected turn in their conversation. "She came up with a plan on the drive here."

Lisa listened, a swirl of emotions churning in her chest—emotions she couldn't quite name. She'd never witnessed Selena this vulnerable in all their lives, and though the circumstances were far from ideal, a small, unexpected sense of closeness flickered inside her.

Her heart swelled with a surge of affection, an ache of longing that made her want to show Selena she was there for her, that their bond could reach beyond old misunderstandings and distant interactions.

It was the connection Lisa had always craved, even if it was surfacing under painful circumstances. "Jordan's right," Lisa chimed in, feeling a new wave of protectiveness rise within her. "You really need to leave him. Now, let's figure out how to hide that bruise so the guys won't notice."

Paula quickly agreed. "Yes, before this turns into the nightmare before Christmas."

At Paula's words, Lisa felt a jolt to shield Selena from any further stress. A surprising unity settled among the three of them, binding them together in a cause that moments ago seemed unthinkable.

Lisa and Paula sprang into action, hearts heavy as they helped Selena disguise the bruise beneath makeup. Amid their hushed movements, Lisa leaned in closer to her sister, voice low and tinged with worry.

"Now who else knows?" she asked quietly, her fingers steadying the concealer brush. She had to gauge the extent of this secret, to safeguard Selena's dignity in such a raw moment. Paula, equally focused on the task at hand, shot a quick glance at Selena, a silent look that seemed to echo Lisa's question. They both needed to ensure this incident stayed within their circle.

To their surprise, Selena divulged that their mother, Lila, already knew. A shock of disbelief spiked through Lisa's chest as she absorbed this revelation.

She exchanged a tense look with Paula, her mind racing over what that might mean—did Mom confront Richard? Would Dad find out next?

Still seething at the sight of Selena's black eye, Lisa blurted out in frustration, "I could get one of my guy friends to go kick Richard's butt." The words, punctuated by raw anger, tumbled out before she could restrain them. She'd do anything to defend her sister, no matter how tenuous their bond had been up until now.

Just as the words left her lips, their brother Bo walked into the room, stopping short at the sight of the three startled women. The tail end of Lisa's sentence hung in the air, prompting his immediate curiosity.

"Kick who's butt?" he asked, his brow furrowing as he scanned their faces, trying to make sense of the tense atmosphere.

Selena moved quickly, slipping her sunglasses back on—a reflexive attempt that Lisa immediately recognized as hiding the bruise. Lisa and Paula both stepped forward, urging Bo to leave.

"Bo, please, not right now," Paula said, her voice trembling. Her eyes darted between him and Selena, a silent plea for him to back out.

Lisa, just as rattled, added, "This isn't your business, Bo!". She noticed the way his gaze lingered, baffled by their abrupt shift in tone.

"Okkkaaaayyyyy," he mumbled. Confusion clouded his expression as he slowly backed out of the doorway. Lisa watched him hesitate for a moment, his hand trailing on the doorknob, before he finally retreated down the hall.

A pang of guilt flickered through Lisa at the sight of his bewilderment, but there was no time for second-guessing. Their priority was to keep Selena's secret—and her bruised face—out of sight.

Lisa watched as Bo lingered by the doorway, clearly unsettled by the tense exchange. He shot them a final glance, brow knit with confusion, before disappearing into the hallway.

As the door clicked shut, Lisa's shoulders sagged with relief—yet a twist of unease coiled in her gut. She could only imagine the questions now brewing in Bo's head. Meanwhile, Paula discreetly rummaged through her purse. Lisa noticed the concerned furrow of her sister-in-law's brow as she fished out a pair of thick-rimmed, clear-lens glasses. With a gentle sigh, Paula offered them to Selena.

"Here," Paula murmured, her voice trembling with empathy. "Wearing sunglasses indoors is just too obvious. But these have a nice, thick rim. Between the make-up and these glasses, it'll help conceal it. No one will notice."

The air hung heavy as the three women exchanged anxious glances. Lisa's pulse thudded at the thought of what might happen if someone discovered Selena's secret—that the bruise came from her own husband's hand. Still, they seemed united in the unspoken pact to protect one another.

Lisa looked from Selena's bruised eye to Paula's makeshift solution, a small flicker of hope sparking in her chest. Paula's clear frames offered a sliver of comfort, a band-aid for a situation that felt far too big to hide. Yet in that moment, Lisa knew they would do whatever it took to keep Selena safe—at least until they could figure out what came next.

Chapter Sixteen

Henry

Cake & Cliff Notes

In the heart of his familial haven, Henry—ever the seasoned patriarch—set in motion a covert cake operation for his eager grandchildren. A mischievous twinkle flashed in his eye as he beckoned Josh, the youngest, to stand guard near the door.

The plan was simple: keep watch for Lila's return. She'd almost certainly protest this dessert-before-dinner escapade, but that was all part of the fun.

Lila, steadfast in her belief that cake belonged strictly after a proper meal, stood in contrast to Henry's own mantra—a slice of cake, at any hour, held the power to remedy just about anything.

Over the years, he'd seen firsthand how the smallest indulgence could ease tears or spark a moment of laughter in the midst of worry. His stance on the transformative power of cake had become an institution in their family—more than mere sweetness, it was a tradition that brought them all closer together.

Cake wasn't just cake; it was a means to connect with his beloved grandchildren, to share not only a bite of something delicious but also bits of hard-earned wisdom—his renowned "cliff notes."

With the promise of secret slices still lingering in the air, Henry nudged his grandchildren to pull out their cell phones and check in on the family's "cliff notes." Angela, adopting a playful air of authority, announced that they'd last tackled cliff note number 32.

Henry nodded, the corners of his mouth curving into a satisfied smile. Another round of his treasured advice would follow soon—right after they made sure to sneak those plates of cake safely out of Lila's sight.

"Alright, folks, Cliff Note Number 33," Henry began, letting his gaze roam over the grandchildren gathered before him. There was a faint buzz of curiosity in the air—he could feel it as tangibly as the scent of the cake cooling on the table.

He paused for a moment, savoring their anticipation before offering his next gem of wisdom. "Bananas are for splitting," he declared, folding his hands as though the phrase alone held the secrets of the universe.

Catching Josh's quizzical expression, Henry chuckled inwardly. He knew this line would spark confusion—and that was half the fun.

"Bananas are for splitting?" Josh echoed, one eyebrow arched in intrigue.

Henry offered a serene nod, elaborating on the seemingly simple maxim. "Yes, indeed. Have one half for yourself, and save the other half. You can enjoy it over cereal, add it to ice cream, or savor it on a piece of toast the following day."

He let the words linger, sensing that beneath their surface simplicity, the grandchildren were catching on to the deeper truth—something about balanced indulgence and the subtle art of pacing oneself.

A lesson in duality and self-control, Henry mused silently, satisfied that he'd planted another seed of thought.

"When you journey," he continued, his voice carrying the calm assurance of someone who had traveled many

roads himself, "whether by foot or by car, spare a moment from the clutches of technology. Sit in the quiet
and let the whispers of God find their way to your heart.
Cliff Note Number 34."

A moment of hush followed, broken only by Angela
and Jordan exchanging playful glances—Henry recognized that good-natured competition. Wonder which of
them will actually set the phone aside first? he thought
with a wry smile.

Meanwhile, Josh, the ever-mischievous one, attempted
to coin his own whimsical cliff note, drawing laughter
from the group. Henry leaned back, content to watch
them revel in this passing moment—a moment that, to
him, felt both lighthearted and profoundly meaningful
all at once.

In Cliff Note Number 35, Henry felt a glimmer of
pride as he shared another piece of his hard-earned wisdom. These lessons always seemed to bloom like wild-
flowers when the grandkids were close by, he mused.

Clearing his throat, he proclaimed, "Surprises, especially when they're wrapped in your time, are the finest
gifts." He paused, noticing how anticipation flickered in

Angel's eyes and a hint of curiosity flashed across Josh's face.

They're listening, he thought, the sparkle in his own gaze growing brighter as he continued. Showing up unexpectedly—like attending someone's basketball game or swinging by with lunch—could mean the world to another person. Henry could see the wheels turning in Angel and Josh's minds.

"Angel, Josh, remember," he said, adopting a playful tone, "these kinds of gestures can go a long way with the ladies."

A mischievous glint danced across his features, and he felt a surge of amusement when his grandsons eagerly nodded in agreement. Across the room, Angela and Jordan exchanged a look that practically screamed whatever. Henry suppressed a chuckle; he knew they had their own ways of interpreting his advice.

"Number 36," Henry continued, letting his gaze drift over to the row of buzzing smartphones. He reminded them of the ever-fading art of answering calls in an era ruled by texts and social media.

"In an era of misinterpreted texts and emojis, picking up a ringing phone can be surprisingly clarifying. Hearing someone's voice—the nuances, the inflections—can prevent misunderstandings." he said.

He paused for effect, allowing the gravity of his words to settle over the group. Then came Cliff Note Number 37, and Henry let his voice settle into a deeper timbre, as though he were about to share a secret.

"Love arrives unannounced," he said, "catching us off guard. And when it does, discern whether that person is deserving of the sanctuary of your heart."

He caught sight of Angel and Angela trading one of their uncanny twin glances—*They're conferring,* Henry thought with a spark of curiosity. *Probably something to do with this bit on love.* He couldn't read their minds, of course, but he sensed a silent dialogue passing between them.

"While death holds physical life in its grasp," Henry continued, recalling a verse that had guided him through his own uncertain days, "love transcends this boundary beyond earthly existence. You'll find this revelation in the Bible where Song of Solomon says: 'For love is as strong as death.'"

His words seemed to linger in the air, and for a moment, the room grew still. Angela's gaze flicked toward her brother once more, and Henry noted a certain softness in her expression, as though she were trying to puzzle out some feeling she hadn't expected.

With a lighthearted grin, Henry broke the hush. "Alright, my fine Grands, who's up for sharing first?" he asked, nudging the conversation along.

Henry nodded to himself as Jordan began to open up about some things she was facing at school, a quiet affirmation rising in his chest. Each soul must find its own path and cultivate its own salvation. That was the real legacy—passing down not just traditions, but truth.

Wisdom, after all, was like a flame. It couldn't be forced. It had to be tended gently, fed with patience, and trusted to catch when the time was right. It comforted him to know that even if they didn't fully understand it now, one day, those cliff notes might guide them through a storm.

Just then, Josh—who had been assigned lookout duty—popped around the corner, eyes wide. "Grandma's coming!" he whisper-yelled, darting back toward the kitchen like a soldier in retreat.

Panic rippled through the room. Plates were shuffled, crumbs swiped, phones pocketed. Henry stifled a laugh as he watched them scramble—part guilt, part joy, all love.

The cake may have been the decoy, but the real treat had already been served.

Chapter Seventeen

LILA

What Love Tries to Hold

"Mayreen, you are not going to have my best friend Tracy upset with me." Lila's voice carried a playful admonishment, but a gentle warmth still laced her tone. She paused in her icing work, looking over at Mayreen with equal measures of motherly care and practical insistence.

"You've visited with Angela," Lila went on, returning her attention to the red velvet cake before her, "and now you have to get back to your Christmas party."

The last swirl of frosting came together beneath Lila's steady hand—a product of years spent perfecting family desserts and holiday spreads.

She took a moment to study Mayreen, noticing the faint hesitance in the younger woman's posture. Poor thing's torn between here and her own party, Lila thought sympathetically.

She recognized that blend of duty and mild apprehension—it was the look of someone who wanted to please everyone at once.

"Now, you make sure and tell Tracy to put this cake in the refrigerator for about an hour to set."

With a baker's practiced assurance, Lila placed the cake into Mayreen's waiting hands. "That icing won't do you much good if it melts all over."

Her gaze lingered on Mayreen, offering a final warm smile. Even in the midst of her own bustling kitchen, Lila felt a pull of affection for this sweet, slightly flustered young woman. Tracy might fret if her cake arrives late, she reminded herself. But it'll be fine—once she tastes it, all will be forgiven.

"And tell your aunts to get in here and help me on your way out," Lila called after Mayreen. She gave a final wave as the young woman left the bustling kitchen, a sweet cloud of cake-scented air following in her wake.

One more set of helping hands gone before I can rope the rest in, Lila mused wryly. She had barely returned her focus to the dishes when Paula breezed in, eyes bright and playful.

"Jordan and Angela said Pops gave them his annual cliff notes. I'm jealous—now it's time for ours."

Hearing mention of "cliff notes," Lila felt a gentle tug of warmth. Henry's snippets of wisdom had become a cherished tradition over the years, weaving the family closer with each passing season. She offered Paula a knowing nod.

"I think I might have a few nuggets for you guys," she said, pleased to carry on the spirit of sharing life lessons. Her gaze grew more serious, however, as she asked, "How are Selena and Lisa getting along?"

A faint line creased her brow. Lord knows I want peace in this family more than anything, she thought, recalling the tension that so often sparked between her daughters.

"You'll be happy to hear they are getting along," Paula replied, a note of relief in her voice. At those words, Lila felt a subtle easing of the tightness in her chest. *Thank God for small mercies*, she reflected, praying silently that this newfound harmony would last.

Lila tried to concentrate on tidying the countertop, but her thoughts kept circling back to Selena. *Did she confide in the girls about the incident?* she wondered. Her musings were interrupted by the arrival of Lisa and Selena, the latter looking a bit strained.

Lisa's cheerful tone cut through the chatter. "Is it almost time to eat, Mom?"

Lila barely registered the question. Her gaze was fixed on Selena, motherly instincts flaring as she discreetly searched Selena's features for any sign of the black eye. Please, Lord, let her be okay, Lila pleaded inwardly, realizing too late she'd left Lisa's question unanswered.

"Oh, yes, yes," she replied hastily, though her attention remained on Selena. "Your Dad said the meat will be ready in half an hour."

An uneasy silence settled, palpable enough to make Lila's pulse quicken. She saw Selena glance around, clearly noticing the tension. Finally, her daughter's quiet voice broke through the hush.

"They know, Momma," she admitted. "I told them what happened."

In an instant, the kitchen's flurry came to a halt. Every eye snapped to Selena, and Lila felt her heart clench. She'd feared this moment, yet part of her was relieved that someone else knew.

In a heartbeat, Lila's protective instincts surged like a wild tide and she began to explain. She insisted this had to be the first time—Selena would never allow herself to be treated so badly. Her voice quivered, betraying a desperation to believe her own reassurances.

Before she could weave a more detailed defense, Lisa cut in with a crisp, unflinching statement: "Mom, you can't explain this away." The reality in Lisa's tone hit Lila like a slap of cold air.

"The evidence is on her face," Lisa added, and Lila felt her heart constrict.

For a moment, Lila stood mute, her certainty unraveling in the face of undeniable truth. She barely had time to gather herself when Selena snapped back at Lisa, her sarcasm hitting hard.

"I'm not sure when you've become so bold, Lisa," Selena retorted, her voice edged with bitterness. "But yes, the evidence is on my face. Thank you so much for pointing that out."

Lisa's face fell, and Lila's own heart ached at the sight. She lamented silently, the fact the Selena even shared it with Lisa was huge.

The entire kitchen seemed to hold its breath, and Lila wished with all her might that she could mend this rift with a few loving words. But right now, everything felt too raw, too real.

"You know what, I can't today." Lisa's voice wavered between anger and exasperation as she turned on her heel, marching straight out of the kitchen.

"Lisa, Lisa!" Paula called after her, concern etched in every syllable. She cast an apologetic glance at Lila before hurrying to catch up. Lila's heart sank—she could practically feel the tension spiking in the wake of Selena's defensive jab.

Lord, I wish they could mend things without tearing each other apart.

From where she stood, Lila heard low voices in the hallway—Lisa's heated tone and Paula's calmer, urging murmurs. She caught fragments of Lisa's raw frustration, something about how everyone always dismissed Selena's biting nature, and then a hushed admonishment from Paula to keep her voice down.

Please, Lord, don't let this get any louder, Lila prayed silently, knowing full well that raised voices had a way of pulling the entire household into the storm. Easing closer to the doorway, she caught the tail end of Paula's urgent plea:

"Now lower your voice, suck it up, and let's get back in here."

Lila pressed a hand to her chest, feeling the anxiety twist in her gut. If they keep at this, the whole dinner could unravel. She took a steadying breath, readying herself for when they returned. Whatever bitterness was brewing, Lila knew she'd have to find a way to guide them back into harmony—or, at the very least, keep the peace until the meal was served.

Lisa stepped back into the kitchen, shoulders drawn tight, eyes clouded with a fire Lila could almost feel. She's still burning with anger, Lila realized, forcing herself to keep busy arranging serving bowls and utensils as though nothing had shattered their fragile moments earlier.

Maybe if she acted calm, the storm would blow over—but inside, her nerves were anything but settled.

Paula threw Lisa a pointed glance, a silent plea for restraint, and Lila caught the uneasy exchange. Yet Lisa's frustration clearly still simmered.

"So we're going to act as if nothing is going on?" she demanded, voice tight with suppressed emotion.

Lila's heart clenched. She wanted to tell Lisa they would address everything—eventually—but the words refused to surface. Instead, she offered Lisa the same no-nonsense look that once quelled a tantrum in their younger years. Enough, that gaze said, recalling days when a single glance could restore a semblance of order.

Without waiting for Lisa's reaction, Lila spun toward the kitchen window, her anxiety spiking at the thought of Henry and the other men overhearing. She peered outside, relieved to see them still engrossed in their own conversation around the grill. Thank God they haven't noticed, she thought, heart pounding.

Behind her, the rush of water signaled Lisa scrubbing her hands with a kind of desperate intensity. Lila kept her back turned, swallowing the urge to say something comforting.

Lord, please let us get through this meal before everything spills over again, she prayed silently, bracing herself for whatever came next.

A tense hush hung in the kitchen until Selena, looking strained, tried to divert everyone's attention. "Do you want the mashed potatoes in the porcelain dish or the glass dish, Mom?" she asked, voice unsteady.

Before Lila could answer, Lisa cut in, her tone laced with sarcasm. "I'm sure you'll be taking some home to Richard."

Lila bristled. She couldn't let this spiral further. With a single, firm word, she silenced Lisa's jab.

"Stop."

The command carried more authority than she intended, but the moment called for it. Sensing the atmosphere grow heavier still, Paula jumped in.

"So, uhm, how about those nuggets of wisdom, Mom Franklin?" she offered, voice higher than usual—an obvious attempt at redirection.

Lila seized the opportunity. She motioned to the bowl of mashed potatoes nestled over a pot on the stove, explaining how the gentle steam kept them warm without drying them out—a simple trick she'd perfected over years of holiday meals.

Selena and Paula, grateful for any change in topic, marveled at the simple yet ingenious method. Lila accepted their praises with a subdued smile, aware that they were all just trying to hold things together.

Even so, Lila's gaze flicked to Lisa, who offered a tight, forced grin that didn't reach her eyes. She's still simmering, Lila thought, recognizing that there was more anger than she could soothe in this moment.

But Lisa said nothing further, and Lila chose not to press her. They would have time—she hoped—to speak honestly later, when tempers weren't so raw.

For now, Lila carried on—doling out culinary guidance and gentle smiles—trying to soften the strain with timeworn traditions. But beneath the familiar clatter of spoons and soft hum of conversation, she felt the undercurrent of tension still threading through the room.

She stirred and smiled, but her spirit remained unsettled. And as the family busied themselves with preparations, a quiet pang of longing rose up within her:

Lord, please let us find a way back to real peace, not just appearances.

Yet she tucked that prayer deep and continued stirring, the comforting warmth of the kitchen doing little to dispel the unresolved strain that lingered in the air.

CHAPTER EIGHTEEN

THE COUSINS

UNHEARD WHISPERS

J ordan shifted in the uncomfortable folding chair nestled in her grandparents' living room, nearly hidden by the high-backed sofa. From her vantage point, she could see the women bustling in the kitchen through the open archway of the hallway. If she glanced to her left, she also glimpsed the men outside in the backyard, their voices blurring into a muffled hum through the window.

They never realize how much we hear, she thought mockingly. Beside her, Josh tossed down a red Uno card with a confident flick of his wrist, his smirk hinting at being the overlooked youngest.

"They never realize we're usually sitting somewhere in the room," he remarked, nodding toward the tension drifting in from the kitchen.

Jordan's lips quirked in agreement echoing the thought that had just crossed her mind. She felt the gentle warmth radiating from the nearby fireplace, but the faint chill snaking along the floor reminded her how easily she and Josh faded into the background when the adults were around.

"Just because we're the *kids* of the family," she said, using air quotes with exaggerated sarcasm, "they think we don't know what's going on."

Josh chuckled softly, his eyes flicking to Jordan's as though sharing a private joke.

"Right. I'm in ninth grade, you're a sophomore. We know everything."

His playful pride made Jordan grin. In truth, she sometimes wished she didn't notice all the things adults tried to keep hidden. Yet she and Josh had learned long ago that silence and a good hiding spot could reveal more than anyone realized.

The worn cards felt smooth against Jordan's fingers as she drew her next one. She was about to tease Josh back when he spoke again, quieter this time, eyes full of concern.

"Your dad... did he hit your mom?"

The question was gentle, yet its weight pressed heavily on Jordan's chest. As she lowered her head, a cloud of sadness veiled her face. Hesitation tightened her throat, mirroring the knot of shame that formed behind her eyes.

"Yes," she said quietly. "He did."

Saying the words aloud made it all feel heavier. She clenched her Uno cards, afraid to meet Josh's gaze.

A sympathetic sigh escaped him.

"I'm sorry that happened," he said softly, a brief hesitation showing his distress. "He must have really lost control."

Jordan swallowed hard, her gaze drifting to the flickering fireplace nearby. The warmth on her face contrasted sharply with the chill she felt inside.

"He treats my mom pretty bad," she admitted, her voice quavering. "And it's time for us to leave. He needs counseling or something... my mom doesn't deserve that."

Silence settled between them, broken only by the distant rattle of dishes from the kitchen. Josh's brow furrowed.

"Geez," he muttered, shaking his head. "And these adults tell us how to act..."

She caught his eyes flicking down at the Uno deck, his frustration coming off in waves. But when he spoke next, his voice was steady, almost comforting.

"You know what's crazy? I miss your dad. Just because he did something bad doesn't mean we stop loving him. Maybe we should pray God will change him."

Jordan felt tears threaten at the corners of her eyes, and she quickly blinked them away. Of all responses, she hadn't expected compassion for her father.

"You're right," she breathed, a fragile hope taking root inside her. "I still love my dad."

Josh gave a small nod, his own expression lighter. "Of course you do. He can change if he wants to."

Jordan's lips curved into the faintest smile.

"Wow, Josh, you're like a little guru," she teased, letting out a breath she hadn't realized she was holding. "And yeah—he can change, if he really wants to."

The moment's tenderness lingered between them, easing some of Jordan's burden. Resting her elbows on her knees, she posed the question, hoping to match the openness Josh had just offered her.

"So how are your parents doing?"

Josh exhaled, his gaze dropping to the small stack of cards in his hand.

"Their divorce was final about six months ago," he said, voice low but steady. "But honestly, my mom's doing pretty good. She used to be super grumpy—like, all the time—and now she's... actually kind of cool. Weird, right? I guess the divorce helped."

He let out a soft chuckle that hovered somewhere between relief and regret, and Jordan couldn't help but offer him a thoughtful tilt of her head.

"Do you want them to get back together?" she asked, curious about how he really felt behind the forced laugh.

Josh paused, cards fidgeting between his fingers.

"I'm not sure," he admitted. Then, a line of worry creased his brow. "My dad's trying to, like... win her back. But he's going about it all wrong."

Jordan arched an eyebrow in mild disbelief. The last time she'd overheard her mom talking to her Uncle Bo, he wasn't speaking too highly of Aunt Trinity.

"Draw two!" Jordan suddenly announced, throwing down her own card with a grin.

Josh let out a loud groan, rolling his eyes as he reached for the pile.

"Ugh, thanks a lot," he said, though a smile tugged at his lips. He jerked his head dismissively, returning to the subject.

"Honestly, those two have no business being together right now. If Dad keeps this up, Mom's gonna hate his guts."

Jordan drew in a gasp, "Oh no," she said, in an exaggerated tone that made Josh smirk. He leaned closer, lowering his voice with a mischievous glint in his eye.

"But get this—it's not all bad. They're in this weird competition about who can buy me the best stuff. Dad shows up with something new, then Mom tops it... It's kind of awesome," he confessed, stifling a laugh.

Jordan couldn't help but join in. Despite the heavy issues swirling among the adults, at least the two of them could still find these small moments of ridiculous humor.

A gentle click from the living room door made them glance up mid-laugh. Angel stepped inside, shrugging off his jacket. The light from outside enveloped him, highlighting his features, and Jordan realized how much he and Angela resembled each other as she set her cards down to greet him.

"Hey, guys," he greeted, nodding at the makeshift card table.

Jordan tilted her head, letting a mischievous grin curl at the corners of her mouth.

"Your shirt isn't even that tight," she teased, recalling the fuss his mom had made earlier.

"Yeah," Josh chimed in, eyes darting from his last Uno card to Angel's waistband. "The way your mom was talking, I was expecting something painted on."

With a triumphant flourish, he slapped down his card and shouted, "The King of Uno!"

Angel puffed up his shoulders, showing off his muscles, brushing off their jokes. Jordan knew him well enough to sense he wasn't about to let any offhand comments from his mother sour his mood. He forced a laugh and closed the distance to the table, pulling out a chair

"Count me in," he said, settling in beside them. "So... what did I miss?" He paused, glancing around the room before casually adding, "I saw Mayreen walking back to Aunt Tracy's. Anybody know why?"

Jordan froze, her heart thumping at the thought of explaining exactly what she and Josh had been talking about moments before. She shot him a quick, pleading look. *Please don't bring it up,* she silently conveyed with a widening of her eyes. Luckily, Josh picked up on her unspoken warning and shifted gears without missing a beat.

"So where's the girlfriend, Angel? I've heard she's really hot," Josh said, a teasing edge in his grin.

Angel's eyebrows arched in mock offense. "Watch it," he warned, but the hint of a grin showed he was amused. He tossed the previous question aside and cleared his throat, clearly opting for a new topic.

"Anyway, what are you two up to this summer? I'm looking to hire some people."

Jordan offered Angel a questioning look, curiosity piqued. She could still feel a warm flutter of relief that Josh had sidestepped any mention of her dad. Whatever Angel was about to say, she welcomed the distraction—and the chance for a fresh hand of cards.

Angel drummed his fingers on the tabletop, excitement evident in his posture as he began explaining his latest venture.

"The car wash should be finished in 3 to 4 months," he announced, his voice brimming with pride. "I'd love to bring you guys on board—earn some extra cash if you want.

Jordan's heart gave a little leap at the prospect. She might have just spilled some heavy truths, but the idea of a new job and real income offered a welcome distraction.

"That'd be fantastic," she blurted, unable to hide her enthusiasm. A job meant freedom—and maybe even a chance to help her mom in ways she hadn't yet considered.

Josh gave an approving nod. "Sounds good," he said, his eyes flicking between Angel and the half-finished Uno deck. "I'll talk to my dad about it. He's been on my case about responsibility, so maybe this will shut him up."

Before Jordan could offer more thoughts, a comforting, spicy-sweet aroma wafted into the living room. She glanced up to see Angela slipping in, balancing a cardboard tray brimming with steaming cups.

"Okay, guys," Angela announced, the warmth in her tone matching the coffee's fragrance. "Your orders are here."

Jordan's stomach rumbled at the heavenly scent. *I didn't realize how chilly it felt in here until I smelled something hot and sweet*, she thought, gratefully accepting the cup Angela handed over.

A swirl of holiday spice and rich espresso curled into her nose as she took the first cautious sip. Angel, apparently noticing that he hadn't been included in the coffee run, pointed playfully at the empty space in front of him.

"Hey, where's mine, Uno?" he demanded with a lop-sided grin.

Angela rolled her eyes at her twin, setting down the last few cups. "You weren't here when I took orders," she countered, eyebrows arched in a mock-scold.

Jordan raised her cup in a playful toast, letting the cozy glow of the fireplace illuminate the swirl of whipped cream perched on top. With a quick flick of her tongue, she scooped up a soft cloud of sweetness. The warmth of the coffee mingled perfectly with the lightheartedness that had settled over the group.

"I'm loving that you wear makeup now," she said to Angela, making sure her voice carried genuine admiration. "It looks so good. Will you do mine sometime?"

Angela's eyes sparkled under the gentle light of the lamps overhead. "Of course," she replied with a teasing smirk. "You might regret that, though. I have a tendency to go full glam when I do other people's makeup."

Jordan laughed, imagining the outrageous lashes and shimmery eyeshadow Angela might apply. Across the table, Josh chimed in, tilting his cup in acknowledgment.

"Yeah, you're all dolled up," he teased. "Looking pretty, Angie."

A subtle flush spread across Angela's cheeks, but before she could respond, Angel tapped his fingers on the table and looked at his twin with a suspicious smirk.

"Didn't you tell me you never had time for makeup with your schedule?" he asked, his tone laced with just enough skepticism to make Jordan's ears perk up.

Angela shrugged, eyes flicking from her brother's probing stare back to her coffee. "It's winter break," she pointed out, as though reminding him of a simple fact. "I finally have a little time for myself—don't worry, I'll be back to normal once school starts."

Jordan sipped her latte, watching the silent exchange of looks between the twins. Before the silence stretched too long, Uncle Bo and Darren appeared in the living room, each carrying a small folding table and extra chairs. A playful grin lit Uncle Bo's face the moment he caught the aroma of fresh coffee.

"Is that coffee I smell?" he asked, setting the table down with an exaggerated sniff.

Angela's face lit with sudden enthusiasm—an enthusiasm Jordan found oddly timed. Angela snatched a cup from the end table, her voice carrying just enough brightness to turn heads.

"Oh, Darren," she called out, projecting slightly so he'd hear her from across the room. "I got you a double chocolate chip frappe, no drizzle on top."

Jordan saw Uncle Bo freeze for the briefest second before turning around, eyebrows arched. Angel also straightened, shooting a curious look Angela's way. Darren glanced back over his shoulder, setting the extra chairs against the wall.

"Thanks," he said, striding toward Angela. His tone was calm, but Jordan noticed a flicker of surprise in his eyes—like he hadn't expected her to announce this in front of everyone.

He reached for the cup with a nod of gratitude. "I appreciate it," Darren continued, "though I guess you're trying to wean me off the drizzle?"

"Where'd that come from?" he teased sarcastically. "I'm her twin, and she didn't even think of me?"

Jordan felt the mood shift, a slight chill creeping in despite the steady warmth from the fireplace. She had a feeling Angel wasn't entirely joking. Across the table, she saw his eyes flick toward Darren and then back to Angela, as though sizing up the situation.

Uncle Bo cleared his throat, stepping in before tension could mount.

"Hey, Angie," he said, affecting a lighthearted tone, "you got anything left over for your dear old uncle? Or is it just certain folks who get the VIP treatment?"

Angela's cheeks turned pink, and she let out a nervous laugh. "Neither of you were around when I took orders," she explained, doing her best to sound casual. "Honestly, I would've grabbed more if I knew you all wanted something."

Jordan took a careful sip of her latte, noting how Darren definitely hadn't been around for the coffee run either. She felt a flutter of unease at the unspoken question: *Why did Angela specifically think of him?*

Better change the subject, fast, Jordan thought, letting her gaze flick between the twins. Angel was still looking at Angela with that slightly suspicious tilt to his head, and Angela was clearly trying to maintain her composure.

As if reading Jordan's mind, Angela cleared her throat and addressed Uncle Bo and Darren in one swift pivot. "I spoke with Melissa in the car," she said, words tumbling out in a rush. "She's hoping to get here soon."

A momentary hush fell as Uncle Bo digested this news. Then his shoulders relaxed, and he chuckled at Angela.

"That's good to hear—though next time, remember the drizzle," he teased with a wink, pointing at Darren's coffee cup. "Strike one for you, Angie."

Jordan watched him clap Darren on the shoulder, guiding him toward the hall that led to the garage. Darren hesitated just long enough to give Angela a conspiratorial wink.

"Good looking out," he murmured.

Just then, Josh launched out of his chair with a triumphant whoop.

"UNO!" he shouted, waving his final card like a prize. "That's how it's done, folks—I'm the king of Uno!"

The sudden outburst made Jordan laugh aloud, relief flooding her chest as though someone had opened a window to let fresh air in. She watched Angela's shoulders lose some of their tension, and even Angel shifted his stance, rolling his eyes good-naturedly at Josh.

Jordan gathered the scattered cards, a small smile tugging at her lips. For now, Josh's perfectly timed interruption was exactly what they all needed.

CHAPTER NINETEEN

BO & DARREN

TANGLED THREADS

B o nudged aside a stack of dusty boxes, clearing a path in his parents' cluttered garage. A single overhead bulb buzzed faintly, casting shadows across the cement floor. He could just make out a faint whiff of old paint mixed with motor oil—the familiar, musty scent he'd grown used to over the years.

"Should be around here somewhere," he said, voice echoing against the concrete walls. "I'm sure we stashed those board games back by the holiday decorations."

Behind him, Darren shifted a rusty toolbox out of the way. Their friendship had always been comfortable, but Bo sensed an unspoken tension in the air. Maybe it was the conversation they'd started—or the fact that he felt behind on so many details these days.

"So, how's the mentorship going with Angela?" Bo asked, flipping open one of the boxes. "All that clinical stuff?"

There was a quiet affection in his tone. He couldn't help feeling protective when it came to his niece. Darren glanced over, a small smile forming on his face.

"She's doing well," Darren replied, brushing a cobweb off his sleeve. "Really well, actually. She's got the dedication, and her clinical's look impressive."

Bo nodded, relief warming his chest knowing Angela was thriving. He pried open another box, rummaging through old photo albums and half-deflated sports balls.

"That's great," he said with genuine pride. "She's always been the focused type."

Silence stretched between them, broken only by the scrape of cardboard against concrete. Yet Bo couldn't shake a faint, nagging worry. That odd moment with Angela's coffee—especially the part about "no drizzle"—kept tapping at the back of his mind, as if there was more to it. He cleared his throat and tried to sound casual.

"How often do you, uh, talk to her?"

Despite his easy tone, a spark of concern flared in his gut. *Is Angela really okay?* he wondered, recalling how uncharacteristically flustered she'd seemed earlier.

Darren paused, leaning his elbows against the workbench. "Every day, actually. I keep tabs on her study schedule. Sometimes I find her up at two in the morning, books spread across the kitchen table—gotta remind her how important rest is at this stage of her clinical's, you know?"

Bo looked up, blinking in disbelief. A faint tickle of confusion crawled across his mind. *Hold on,* he thought. *Did he say he finds her up at two a.m.?*

"Remind her to crash?" Bo echoed, struggling to keep his tone casual. "You mean, like... you see her at night?" He didn't intend for his words to sound so pointed, but the implication caught him off guard.

Why is Darren seeing her in the middle of the night at all? he wondered, tugging absently at a loose edge of tape on a nearby box. His heartbeat thudded a little harder against his chest. If Darren was stepping in to ensure she actually slept, it seemed more like a permanent arrangement than the short-term favor they'd discussed several months back.

A chill that had nothing to do with the cold air settled over them. Darren hesitated, rummaging through a stack of puzzle boxes before finally answering.

"Honestly, she's at our place more than her own," he said slowly. "I'd say she stays over about four nights a week."

Bo's stomach tightened. He hadn't thought this was a big deal, but now frustration mixed with concern. It was clear Darren hadn't meant to hide anything—but still, how had this slipped through the cracks?

Bo studied him, his mind racing. *How did we miss this?* He tried to piece it together—he remembered the eviction process had already advanced too far. It was going to take a few days to reverse everything, even with the money. That's when Darren had agreed, as a favor to him, to let her crash there for a bit. Just a few days. And it made sense—Darren and Melissa were her mentors, and with the pressure of clinical's, it seemed like a safe place for her to land while things got sorted out.

Now, doubt crept in. *Was there more going on than she let on?* He'd been so consumed with the fallout from his divorce that he hadn't followed up. Honestly, he thought it had only been a few days at Darren's—something temporary.

He wondered if Sam and Paula even knew she was spending that many nights a week at Darren and Melissa's. Her parents hadn't said much, and no one had made a trip up to San Diego lately. *Maybe everyone just assumed the same thing he did—that she was living at her place.* But clearly, that wasn't the case.

"Look man, I know you didn't do this intentionally. But I don't think my brother Sam and Paula know about this arrangement. You know this isn't smart, right?"

The stark reality of the situation weighed heavily on Bo's mind, stirring a cocktail of worry and a sense of responsibility.

"Dude, what are you implicating?"

Darren blinked, caught off guard. Bo could see it hit him—the way his shoulders tensed, the way he crossed his arms like he was bracing for impact. A charged energy flared between them, and Bo could almost feel the temperature rise as he squared off with his friend.

"You realize this isn't just about letting Angela crash on your couch, right?" Bo snapped, his voice climbing in volume. "Mentoring is supposed to happen in a hospital or an office, not your house. People will talk. You have Angela in there getting your coffee with no drizzle. Man, come on!"

Darren stiffened, crossing his arms. Bo could see the tension rise in him—jaw tight, eyes narrowed.

"You're my best friend," Darren shot back, voice tight with emotion. "I did this as a favor to you. I'm not crossing any lines here. I'm just trying to help her."

Bo pressed his lips together, forcing himself to breathe through his nose to keep his temper in check.

"You helped her out as a favor—for a few days," he said sharply. "Not to let it graduate into her staying there four nights a week. We've talked about how easily things blur when you're working too closely with women at your practice," he reminded Darren, leveling him with a pointed stare.

"Now it's happening under your own roof. And to top it off, my brother doesn't know. If this goes south, it's going to blow up—professionally and personally."

Darren's jaw tensed, and Bo saw his eyes flick toward the floor—like the weight of their past conversations about boundaries had just landed. Bo's words had struck a nerve. He could see it, even if Darren wasn't saying it out loud.

A sudden crunch of gravel drew both their attention to the garage door. Josh appeared, peering around the corner with a cautious expression.

"Uh, dinner's ready," he announced, pausing as though he could feel the charged air between his father and Darren.

"You guys... good? Kinda sounded like an argument."

Bo cleared his throat, forcing his voice into a steadier register.

"We're fine," he said, though annoyance flickered in his eyes. "We'll be right there."

Josh shrugged, darting one last curious look at them. Unable to help himself, he added,

"I know an argument when I see one. I *am* you and Trinity's son."

Darren managed a quiet chuckle, but Bo didn't.

"Boy, get your butt in the house," Bo grunted. "And since when do you call your mother by her first name?"

Before darting away, Josh turned and gave a cheeky wave.

"Bye, Dr. No Drizzle," he quipped.

Bo exhaled, scrubbing a hand over his face.

"That boy..." he muttered, their heads shaking with a shared chuckle.

"We'll finish this later," Bo added, his tone firm. "But I need you to understand—this can't blow up in Angela's face."

Darren gave a slow nod, his own anger retreating.

"I get it," he said more quietly this time. Their gazes met, an unspoken agreement settling between them.

"C'mon," Bo said at last, his voice low. "The Monopoly game is under that shelf, and I'll grab Scrabble. We better get inside." Bo assured Darren he wasn't making accusations so much as looking out for Angela—and for Darren, too.

Even as they gathered the games, Bo's mind churned with plans to fix the situation before it spiraled. The last thing he wanted was to disrupt the family's harmony—especially concerning his brother Sam and his wife Paula.

A resolute determination settled in Bo's gut. He needed to speak with Angela—privately. There were still gaps he couldn't ignore about why she was spending so much time at Darren and Melissa's place when she had her own apartment. He wasn't angry, but he wasn't brushing it off either. Whatever this was—it needed to stop. And it needed to stop now. Angela was clearly crushing on Darren, and he knew it.

CHAPTER TWENTY

HOLIDAY CHARADES

TINSEL & TRUTH

After enjoying a warm holiday meal filled with laughter and comfort food, the family lingered in the grand dining room, ready for more fun.

Tinsel clung to Lisa's hair like festive cobwebs, and from her vantage point in the grand dining room, Lila watched the family gather for a spirited game of charades. The air was alive with the sounds of joyful chatter and the soft hum of holiday music.

In one corner, Lisa took center stage, pantomiming a reindeer with all the grace of a hippo on roller skates. Her makeshift antlers—two spatulas rescued from the kitchen—threatened to topple with each exaggerated prance, drawing peals of laughter.

Lila's eyes softened as she observed the familiar scene. Even Bo, ever the ham, wasn't one to be outdone. He burst into his own flamboyant portrayal of Santa Claus stuck in a chimney.

With a borrowed couch pillow bolstering his belly, each chuckle made it jiggle, while his garland beard seemed to sprout new wisps with every desperate cough.

It was the kind of heartwarming silliness that, for a moment, made the burdens of the year seem far away.

Amidst the merriment, Lila's steady gaze swept over the room. She noted how Josh, ever the keen observer, was silently capturing every detail—especially the way his father, Bo, appeared genuinely happy, unburdened and free.

Yet, even as Bo laughed and played the part of a care-free holiday spirit, Lila sensed something more complex behind his smile.

Bo's laughter felt like a clumsy, overzealous attempt to recapture fleeting moments of happiness. Every hearty chuckle carried echoes of nostalgia and regret—Lila knew her son still hadn't accepted that his marriage was over.

As she glanced back at her mature grandson, Josh, a familiar scripture came to mind: *"you reap what you sow,"* as she saw how he now lent his support and care in return.

For Lila, these moments of apparent cheer were bittersweet: her son was trying desperately to move on, even as the unresolved wounds of a broken marriage quietly haunted him.

As the fire leaped and crackled, its swirling warmth embraced the room, yet beneath the shimmering tinsel and twinkling lights, Lila knew that not every heart was light—some were weighed down by secrets and pain.

Her eyes fell on Selena, who performed the charade of holiday joy with a practiced smile that never quite reached her eyes. Earlier that day, Lila had overheard hushed whispers between Selena and Jordan about escaping the chaos at home—about even seeking refuge in their home.

And yet, when her brothers casually inquired about Richard's whereabouts, none would have guessed that he had struck Selena just hours earlier. Selena's flawless act of normalcy made Lila wonder: *how long had this violence been hidden behind forced smiles?*

As a mother, Lila felt a piercing guilt and a torrent of questions for God: *Why hadn't He revealed this sooner? What if Richard had done something even worse?* So many questions crowded her spirit, even as she remained thankful for the small mercies that had kept them safe.

Then, as God often intercedes in quiet moments, Lila received a revelation: her interceding prayers were the shield preventing Richard from taking Selena's life.

"My, my, my, Lord, I thank You. Open Selena's eyes," she whispered, her heart swelling with gratitude amid the sorrow.

At that moment, laughter erupted in the room as Selena, exasperated with their inability to guess her charade correctly, hopped on one leg and shouted, "Open your eyes!"

Lila sipped her eggnog, its warmth mingling with the sweet spice on her tongue, and she shook her head with a knowing smile. *"You just can't make that up,"* she mused, marveling at how Selena's impassioned outburst had echoed the very words of her silent prayer.

In that fleeting moment, Lila felt a surge of bitter-sweet wonder—a divine confirmation that even amid the chaos, God had a way of speaking directly to the heart.

It had become Lila's habit at every family gathering to observe every detail before everyone left—a ritual she and Henry shared as they later discussed each person's status. This routine not only shaped their prayers but also found its way into the pages of Lila's journal.

There are many untold stories hidden behind each bright smile, Lila thought, a solemn truth mingling with the festive cheer.

Lila's gaze drifted to Jordan, whose quiet isolation amid the revelry tugged at her heart. The specter of violence still cast long shadows on her granddaughter's face, and as she observed her mother's expertise at charades, she could see the contemplation on Jordan's face.

Lila felt the weight of both compassion and resolve. She silently hoped that one day Selena would find the strength to break free from her situation and that Jordan's longing for genuine escape wouldn't remain just a silent wish.

Even as Lila's heart ached for the hidden sorrows in Jordan's eyes, her attention was soon drawn to another unfolding drama as her eyes met Henry's and he nodded towards Angela and Dr. Darren.

There, amidst playful teasing, Angela's hand lingered on Darren's thigh—a delicate, intentional touch that punctuated their shared amusement. Darren tilted his head toward her, and Angela brushed her hair back with a subtle, flirtatious motion.

Lila's eyes, sharp as winter stars, locked with Henry's in a silent exchange. The corners of her mouth curled into a knowing suspicion, echoing the unspoken understanding in Henry's gaze.

Though some might dismiss them as "old" or out of touch, Lila and Henry had weathered countless storms together. Their unspoken communication, honed by years of shared experiences, allowed them to read the room without a word.

When Angela and Darren's fingers brushed while reaching for the same card, Henry's grip tightened imperceptibly on his glass, and Lila's eyebrows arched in silent surprise.

Like seasoned detectives scanning a familiar crime scene, they filed away that small, telling snapshot for future bedroom discussion.

From her seat on the fringes of the conversation, Lila watched Bo's hawk-like eyes dart between Darren and Angela, capturing every subtle cue. She noted how the moment their fingers brushed while reaching for the same card, it seemed to send a silent signal through Bo's vigilant gaze. Angela's constant fussing with her hair confirmed what her son suspected—she was clearly developing a crush.

Lila felt a familiar mix of concern as she observed Bo's protective instinct surge. A young woman infatuated with an older man's status needed careful guidance.

Meanwhile, with a resigned shake of her head tinged with disappointment, Lila watched Sam and Paula—completely oblivious to Angela's crush and the subtle signals it sent. She recalled how Sam had confided in her that, now as empty nesters, Paula was eager to explore new horizons on her own.

Perhaps their own excitement about this newfound freedom had left them too absorbed in their own journey to notice the tender stirrings unfolding between Angela and Angel, Lila thought silently.

"So, Darren, I'm truly disappointed Melissa couldn't make it," Bo remarked, his voice measured but laden with unspoken implications.

At that moment, Selena chimed in with empathy in her tone. "You doctors never catch a break. I know you're happy to have the day off."

Lila listened as their words wrapped around the room. She recognized this as a moment that demanded acknowledgment, and she watched Bo prepare to steer the conversation in a direction he deemed necessary.

"I have a cousin who lives in San Diego—he's here visiting family about fifteen minutes away. He's actually on his way to pick me up. Mrs. Franklin, if you don't mind, I think Melissa would love something home-cooked. If you could spare a plate, I'd love to bring one back for her."

Lila gave a gracious nod. "Of course, dear. We'd be happy to send her something."

"That's so thoughtful—she'd love that," Angela said, her voice light. But Lila had raised enough daughters to recognize when a cheerful tone was covering something else. Lila's mind raced with reflections on the tangled web of family dynamics.

She understood Bo's protective nature, and in that charged moment, she silently resolved to keep a careful watch over these fragile connections. Her intuition warned her that even the smallest, seemingly innocent gesture between a man and a woman could quickly blossom into something far more profound.

After finishing the rest of her eggnog, Lila's eyes followed Angela as she sprang from the couch with determined urgency.

In a flurry of motion, Angela dashed toward the kitchen and began preparing a plate for Darren to take to Melissa—a calculated move that Lila noted was clearly meant to deflect any suspicion of a budding crush.

With an affectionate grin, Lila was pleasantly surprised when Paula mouthed, "Don't give up on love, Lisa; you never know." As the matriarch, Lila had long mastered the art of lip-reading—her children often exchanged whispered secrets that they assumed were hidden from her. Henry gave her another knowing signal with a quick head tilt, urging her to get up and investigate further. Quickly, while the women remained distracted, Lila rose and strolled through the room with a quiet grace, determined to be a little nosy.

Passing near the loveseat where they sat, she caught a glimpse of Lisa's phone. On the screen, an extravagant display of roses—spelling out a message—spread across an image that looked like they'd crawled from Lisa's front lawn.

Lila let out a silent gasp as Paula's eyes darted away—only to quickly meet Lila's in a brief, conspiratorial glance. With a subtle wink, Paula silently acknowledged the secret displayed on Lisa's phone.

Returning to her seat, Lila fixed Henry with a look that clearly said, "I've got something to tell you," as she recognized the gentle affection blossoming on Lisa's face.

Yet, Lila couldn't help but notice that Lisa kept stealing glances at her sister Selena, who remained utterly absorbed in the festivities. Lila sensed a quiet longing in Lisa's eyes—a yearning for a connection deeper than the teasing jabs and superficial banter they exchanged.

I've seen this kind of distance before—walls built over years of silent pain. If only she could tear them down and speak her truth, Lila thought.

Although Lisa laughed and traded girly confidences with her sister-in-law, Lila knew that behind that radiant smile lay a silent plea for the genuine closeness with her real sister.

For Lila, it was a poignant reminder of the fractures in their family—how both her daughters maintained guarded demeanors at the expense of genuine connection.

As the game of charades reached its peak, the atmosphere shifted unexpectedly. Sam—engaged in playful antics alongside Bo and Selena—suddenly walked up to Paula and kissed her deeply, completely oblivious to the watchful eyes of the gathered family. Lila's lips twitched into a fond smile as she noted Bo's playful scolding and the shocked glance that followed, the surprise sending ripples through the room.

Paula, with a tender acknowledgment of her husband's bold gesture, returned the kiss, deepening the moment with affectionate humor.

In an instant, the room erupted with amused whistles and cheers, and laughter soared even higher when Angel, clearly taken aback by the public display, ordered his parents to rein it in.

Angela reentered the room carrying a to-go plate for Dr. Darren, but froze in her tracks at the sight of her parents. "Eww, what are you guys doing?" she exclaimed, her voice tinged with shock—a comment that drew an equally embarrassed retort from Angel.

Laughter soon resumed as Sam proudly exchanged high-fives with Bo and Darren, declaring with a grin, "That's how you keep the fire lit!"

From her quiet vantage point, Lila shook her head and fixed her gaze on Henry. His quiet smile, warm and approving, confirmed the playful spirit of the moment. Then, with a quick clap of his hands that broke through the residual hum of laughter, Henry jumped up from the table and announced, "That's a wrap—y'all don't have to go home, but you gotta get out of here."

A chorus of groans and laughter followed, with a few playful boos and someone tossing a napkin in protest. Bo shouted, "Always shutting it down too early, Pops!" while Josh yelled, "Encore, encore!"

Lila chuckled, her heart swelling at the sound of their laughter. In that instant, she felt the familiar pulse of family chaos mingled with something deeper—a warmth that reminded her how moments like these could brighten even the darkest corners of their lives.

As the soft glow of dwindling lights mixed with the lingering aroma of holiday treats, Lila took it all in. Their Christmas gathering was coming to an end, and she had absorbed every detail.

CHAPTER TWENTY-ONE

PAULA

PERMISSION TO BREATHE

As Paula crossed the threshold into her luxurious suite, a wave of emotion washed over her, mirroring the vast expanse of the ocean that greeted her through the floor-to-ceiling windows. The sight was nothing short of breathtaking—the ocean's turquoise waters stretched as far as the eye could see, merging seamlessly with the endless sky above. But it wasn't just the view that stirred her heart; it was the thoughtful gestures that awaited her within the suite.

Three dozen roses, their petals vibrant against the elegant backdrop of the room, infused the air with their sweet fragrance, enveloping Paula in a sense of warmth and affection. And there, on the polished coffee table, sat a small gift box—its presence a tantalizing promise of delight.

As she sank into the plush sofa, her eyes lingered on the roses and the box before her. She couldn't help but feel a swell of emotion in her chest. Every detail spoke volumes about the lavishness that surrounded her.

Though tempted to open the gift box and card, Paula chose to pause—savoring the stillness and the peace of her surroundings.

Stepping onto the balcony, Paula breathed in the salty breeze, surprised by how warm the railing felt against her palms—even though it was New Year's. In the distance, she could hear the steady rush of waves rolling onto the shore and faint music drifting from a beachside bar. Behind her, the curtains stirred softly, adding to the quiet calm of the unexpectedly mild temperature.

The ocean stretched out endlessly, its surface a mesmerizing mix of blues and greens, shifting and dancing in the golden light of the setting sun. Along the sandy shores, people moved like tiny specks, their laughter and chatter carried on the breeze. Families played and splashed in the gentle waves, children building sandcastles with carefree abandon.

Couples strolled hand in hand along the water's edge, their silhouettes etched against the shimmering expanse of the sea. And there, nestled beneath the shade of a colorful beach umbrella, sat a lone figure—a woman lost in the pages of a book.

As she watched the scene unfold before her, Paula felt a sense of peace settle within her soul. At fifty, she had learned the value of patience—of not rushing headlong into every moment, but rather pausing to fully appreciate the beauty that surrounded her.

And in this moment, as she stood bathed in the soft glow of the setting sun, an undercurrent of guilt tugged at Paula's heart. The sight of Sam's longing gaze as she drove away lingered in her mind.

She couldn't shake the uneasy feeling creeping in. Deep down, she knew that taking this time for herself meant leaving her loved ones behind—and their disappointment still hung in the air, even from miles away.

And then there was her mother's voice, sharp and accusing, replaying in her head. How could she justify her actions—leaving her good husband behind on New Year's Eve, a time meant for celebration and togetherness? The harsh words left her second-guessing every-thing.

The weight of guilt deepened as Paula's thoughts turned to her children's reactions. Angel's teasing words, though meant in jest, stung. "I guess Mom would rather spend New Year's with her boyfriend?"

And then there was Angela—concerned, but with a tone that carried just a touch of judgment. She reminded Paula that she could always talk to her, but then made an offhand comment about how long-term relationships can become boring. That part struck a nerve.

Angela's unexpected suggestion caught Paula off guard—the mere insinuation that it was acceptable for her to feel attraction toward someone new after being with her father for so long really got under her skin.

How could Angela suggest such a thing?

Paula couldn't fathom how Angela—whom she had raised within the biblical teachings of the church—could even entertain the notion that infidelity was somehow permissible. Had she failed as a mother to instill the im-portance of loyalty and devotion in her daughter?

As her own words faded into the quiet, a wave of regret washed over Paula while she stepped back into the room.

Frustration tugged at her. How was it that in a world that praised independence, taking time for herself stirred up so much pushback?

Just as she began to spiral into her thoughts, her phone rang. Paula's heart skipped a beat at the sight of Sam's name on the FaceTime call, his voice a familiar comfort in the midst of her unease.

"Sorry, babe," he said softly, his words a soothing balm to her troubled mind. "I couldn't wait. By my calculations, you should already be in the room."

Relief flooded through Paula, grateful for his understanding. "You're not upset?" she asked timidly, her voice laced with uncertainty.

"Wait a minute, Paula," Sam interjected, his tone firm yet gentle. "Are you beating yourself up? Stop it right now."

Paula lowered her eyes from the screen, feeling a pang of guilt.

"Look at me," Sam urged. "You deserve this."

With a renewed sense of confidence, Paula lifted her head, meeting Sam's gaze with a small smile.

"Thank you," she whispered, her voice choked with emotion. "I needed to hear that."

Sam's understanding and support in that moment encapsulated all the reasons why she loved him so deeply. Their relationship wasn't just built on romantic love; it was fortified by a profound friendship that served as the bedrock of their marriage. In times of uncertainty and self-doubt, it was Sam who grounded her, reminding her of her strength.

As he shared his plans to reconnect with old friends over a round of golf, Paula couldn't help but feel blessed by his willingness to nurture their individual interests while still championing each other's growth.

As Sam blew her a kiss and bid her farewell to enjoy her time and open his gift, Paula felt her heart swell. Excited, she walked back to the foyer and picked up the box sitting beneath her beautiful flowers. With trembling hands, she opened the card, her breath catching in her throat as she read the words inscribed within.

The note, written in her husband's familiar handwriting, resonated with a tenderness that touched Paula's heart. It read:

My dearest Paula,

As you embark on this journey of self-discovery, know that you do so with my love and support. You are deserving

*of this time to nurture your soul and find peace within
yourself.*

*I noticed the way your eyes sparkled when you admired
that necklace at Costco, and I couldn't resist the opportunity
to bring a piece of that joy to your trip.*

*Wear it proudly, my love, and remember that no matter
where you go, I am always with you—heart and soul.*

With all my love,   Sam

Holding the note to her chest, Paula felt tears well up
in her eyes once again. Sam's words were a quiet beacon,
reminding her that everything was going to be okay. With
a blend of gratitude and awe, she reached for the small
midnight-blue velvet box, her fingers trembling as she
untied the delicate ribbon.

Inside lay the necklace she'd been admiring, its beauty
dazzling in the room's soft glow. Tears that had pooled in
her eyes now spilled over, tracing a path down her cheeks
as she gently clasped it in place.

Admiring her husband's love wrapped around her
neck in the mirror, Paula caught a glimpse of the
brochures scattered around her suite.

Determined to embrace the spirit of adventure on her
solo trip, she crossed the room and picked them up, a

flutter of anticipation stirring within her. She knew she wanted her weekend to be more than just indulgent spa treatments; she craved experiences that would feed her soul and create lasting memories.

With growing excitement, she flipped through the options, each one holding the promise of adventure and discovery. And then, among all the offerings, one activity in particular captured her imagination:

"Cooking While Cruising."

The description painted a picture of culinary delight—a small class led by a skilled chef, followed by the opportunity to savor the meal on the deck, overlooking the picturesque coastline.

The idea resonated deeply with Paula. It wasn't just about learning to cook—it was about the camaraderie of sharing a meal, the joy of discovering new flavors, and the beauty of connecting with others in a meaningful way.

With a smile tugging at her lips, this was exactly the kind of experience she had been craving—a chance to step outside her comfort zone. As Paula contemplated joining the tour, a flicker of hesitation danced in her mind.

The idea of trading the quiet comfort of her suite for a group of unfamiliar faces made her hesitate. But then, with a steadying breath and a spark of courage, Paula picked up the phone, her fingers buzzing with anticipation.

The concierge's voice was warm and reassuring as he let her know there was just one spot left on the tour—and she'd need to be in the lobby within forty-five minutes. Glancing at her watch, a spark of excitement flickered to life. She hadn't done something this spontaneous since she was a teenager.

Rummaging through her luggage, Paula's hands moved with purpose as she pieced together the perfect nautical-inspired ensemble. Each item was carefully chosen, and she envisioned herself blending seamlessly into the ambiance of the excursion.

With a flourish, she draped an elegant cardigan around her neck, its soft fabric offering both warmth and style. As she admired her reflection in the mirror, a sense of confidence surged through her. This was more than just an outfit—it was a statement of her readiness to connect with the world around her.

In what felt like no time at all, forty-five minutes had almost passed. Ready for something new, Paula made her way to the lobby, anticipation bubbling in her chest. She knew that this decision marked the beginning of something truly extraordinary. And with each step she took, she felt herself growing bolder, more resilient, and more alive than ever before.

CHAPTER TWENTY-TWO

LILA & JORDAN

FAMILIAR ROUTINE

L ila eased her car into the long line of parents waiting
to pick up their children, the gentle purr of engines
blending with snippets of radio chatter from neighbor-
ing vehicles. She caught the distant thump of a bass line
from someone's open window and the faint rumble of
an impatient driver honking far behind her. Despite the
noise, a wave of nostalgia washed over her, warm and
comforting, like stepping into a pair of well-worn shoes.

It's been so long since I've done this, she thought, feeling a
tug at her heart as she recalled the countless mornings and
afternoons spent ferrying her own children to and from
school. It was the rhythm of a life that had once defined
her days, and now she felt its embrace again.

As she inched her sedan forward, she imagined her own children in the backseat, memory superimposing the soft echoes of their voices onto the here and now. In her mind's eye, she saw herself reciting the family's daily prayer:

"Lord, we thank You for letting us see another day. This is the day that the Lord has made; we shall rejoice and be glad in it." Her lips curled into a gentle smile as she recalled how, back then, her children would chime in on cue:

"Amen. Lord, we ask for and receive grace for this day."

The recollection brought a sense of awe. *Even after everything, that old routine still comforts me,* she mused, fingers tapping absently on the steering wheel. The line crawled forward. Lila glanced at the sprawling high school building—a mixture of beige walls, bright murals, and glass windows—bathed in the waning afternoon light.

Students in clusters darted across the sidewalks, their laughter and excited chatter carrying on the breeze. A sense of calm settled over Lila. *Routine is a gift,* she thought. *Especially now.*

Her thoughts drifted to Jordan, her granddaughter who had come to live with her and Henry after Selena chose to return to Richard. The weight of that decision pressed down on Lila's heart. *I still can't believe my daughter stayed with him,* she lamented silently, recalling the bruises Selena had tried so hard to hide. *God, protect her. Please.*

Jordan, on the other hand, had emerged from the turbulence with a surprising resolve. She'd insisted on moving in with Lila and Henry, seeking the safety and love of her grandparents' home.

Henry hadn't entirely understood at first—Lord knows that man hates changing a routine—but eventually, Selena worked out a story about Jordan needing a calmer environment for her studies. *At least she's here with us,* Lila reminded herself. *She's safe.*

Night after night, worry and prayers had occupied Lila's thoughts, especially now that the truth of Richard's abuse remained a secret known only to the women in the family.

Even Henry was still in the dark about what had truly pushed Jordan to move in. Lila exhaled slowly, as if she could release the tension tightening her shoulders. *Sele-*

na, what are you thinking? she wondered. *How could you go back to him?*

She moved up in line once more, eyes scanning for Jordan among the students trickling out through the school's front gates. Lila recalled the changes she'd seen in Jordan: the once-sociable teenager had drawn inward, focusing most of her time on cooking experiments with Lila or talking over coffee with Henry in the mornings. At least she's bonding with us, Lila reassured herself, though she grieved the carefree days Jordan used to have with her friends.

The school doors swung open wider, releasing a new group of chatting students. Lila's gaze latched onto a familiar figure stepping outside—tall, with a bright smile that seemed to warm the chilly air. Her heart soared.

Jordan spotted her and waved, weaving through the remaining cars with quick, light steps. As she slid into the passenger seat, her beaming expression faded into a thoughtful frown. Lila's heart did a little flip, instantly sensing something was off.

"Hey, Grandma." Jordan's words came softly, tinged with unease.

Lila studied her granddaughter's face, noticing the slight crease in her brow. "Hey, sweetheart," she said, gently squeezing Jordan's hand. "How was your day?"

Jordan hesitated, her eyes flicking to the dashboard before meeting Lila's. "My dad showed up with lunch today."

Lila's breath caught. She gripped the steering wheel tighter, knuckles whitening. "Richard showed up at your school?"

Jordan nodded, eyes full of a careful mix of apprehension and lingering hope. "He... brought me lunch. He said he wanted to apologize. Said he's trying to be a better man."

The engine idled quietly beneath them, but Lila could hear her own pulse thudding in her ears. *Does Selena know?* she wondered, though she suspected the answer.

"Were... were you scared?" she asked gently.

"At first," Jordan admitted, voice trembling. "You know I haven't seen him since Christmas. But... he seemed sincere, Grandma." She paused, staring down at her hands. "I want to believe him."

"Oh, Jordan." Compassion flooded Lila's chest. She reached out, brushing a stray hair from her granddaughter's forehead. "Did he say anything else?"

Jordan shrugged. "Not much. Just kept saying sorry. Gave me some money, too—but I told him I didn't want him just showing up like that again."

She swallowed hard, as if the memory still churned in her. "Mom knew he was coming, but she didn't tell me."

Lila's annoyance flared. So Selena did know. She glanced down at her phone, the screen lighting up with Selena's name—a call she had no intention of answering at the moment.

"Well," Lila sighed, "He is your father, Jordan, but I wish your mother had warned us."

Jordan pressed the folded bills into Lila's hand. "Please, use it for groceries or something. I don't want his money."

Lila's heart squeezed with love for her granddaughter's unselfishness. "You are such a sweet child," she murmured, giving Jordan a small, proud smile. "Let's go shopping."

Jordan's eyes widened. "Grandma, really?"

"Really," Lila insisted, flicking on her turn signal as she steered them out of the school parking lot. "Sometimes a little retail therapy can help clear the mind."

Moments later, they pulled into the crowded mall parking lot. A swirl of chatter and car horns met them as Lila found a spot. Selena's name flashed on her phone screen again, but she silenced it. *I'll deal with her later.*

"You know what, Jordan?" she said, turning toward her. "Before we go in, let's pray."

Jordan nodded. Inside the quiet car, they bowed their heads.

"Father," Lila whispered, "thank You for keeping Jordan safe. If Richard really wants to change, help him. And please... protect Selena."

She squeezed Jordan's hand, prompting her to finish the prayer.

"Lord, we ask for and receive Your grace," Jordan echoed.

They stepped out into the crisp afternoon air. The scent of coffee drifted from the mall entrance, and Lila pulled Jordan close. *We'll figure this out together,* she thought.

Inside, the mall buzzed with shoppers and newly hung Valentine's decorations. When Jordan paused at a sneaker display, Lila smiled. "That's what we're here for."

While Jordan browsed, Lila's eyes caught a rack of sweaters. Henry had been complaining about the cold—he could use a new one. She reached for a forest-green one but hesitated. *How can I buy him a gift and still keep this secret?*

Jordan noticed her expression. "You okay?"

Lila held up the sweater. "Think your grandfather would wear this?"

Jordan chuckled. "If you picked it, definitely."

After paying for the shoes and sweater, they weaved through the crowd, the scent of cinnamon pretzels thick in the air. Lila's phone buzzed again—Selena. She ignored it.

Jordan stiffened as a group of teens from her school passed by. Without a word, she turned in the opposite direction.

"You don't want to say hi?" Lila asked gently.

Jordan shook her head. "I'd rather just stay with you."

Lila saw the pain behind her granddaughter's eyes. This used to be the girl who couldn't stay off the phone with friends.

"Honey, are you embarrassed about living with us?"

"They don't know why I moved, but I'm sure they suspect something. I just... don't fit anymore."

"You've got nothing to be ashamed of," Lila said. "You're doing your best."

They found a quiet bench near a fountain. Jordan sank down and traced circles on the sneaker box. "It's not fair. Mom and Dad should figure this out—not me. I shouldn't feel guilty."

"No, you shouldn't," Lila agreed. "But your mother loves you. She's just... not ready."

Jordan looked up, eyes full of worry. "What if he hurts her again? Grandma, I'm scared."

Lila hugged her tightly. "I'm scared too. But we keep praying and trusting God to protect her."

After a long pause, Jordan whispered, "Do you think Grandpa will ever find out?"

Lila exhaled. "Maybe. Part of me thinks he should. But your mama asked me not to tell him. She's afraid of what he might do."

Jordan nodded slowly. "Do you feel bad for not telling him?"

"I do. We've never kept secrets like this. But I'm praying things will change."

Jordan squeezed her hand. "I'm sorry Gran."

Lila smiled. "I'm just glad you're safe with us."

They stood and headed for the exit, their bags in hand. The air outside was brisk, a welcome change from the crowded mall.

"Thanks, Grandma," Jordan said. "For everything."

"Always, baby girl." Lila kissed her forehead. "Let's go home. You can show Grandpa your new shoes—though don't be surprised if he jokes that we emptied the bank."

Jordan laughed, and the sound filled Lila's heart with hope. There were still unanswered questions and heavy truths, but one thing remained: God was in control, and love held them all together.

Chapter Twenty-Three

LISA

Valentine's Day

With each delicate movement, Lisa's fingers traced the fabric of her chosen dress—a soft reminder of the journey she was about to embark upon. The mirror reflected a mix of uncertainty and determination in her eyes as she silently wrestled with lingering doubts.

Would this really be different?

Liam's persistence had steadily chipped away at the walls she had meticulously built. Since Christmas, his gestures had been a quiet symphony of devotion, each bouquet a note in his growing affection.

Now, as January bid farewell and February beckoned with the promise of blossoming love, Lisa found herself at the crossroads of her own desires. After fastening the final button, she took a deep breath.

With hesitant eyes, she skimmed the delicate black lace of her dress, in her reflection Lisa saw not just her own image, but the reflection of someone yearning to break free from the confines of fear. Each thread held a glimpse of the woman she had been and the one she was becoming.

When the doorbell chimed, a jolt of anticipation surged through her veins. With trembling hands, she approached the door and turned the doorknob.

There he was—bathed in the light of the sun, his presence commanding the very air around him. Liam, the man who had occupied her thoughts and dreams since Christmas, stood before her as a vision of strength and allure that threatened to steal her away.

They had spoken countless times over the phone and exchanged brief words on the court, but nothing could have prepared her for his presence—now in her home.

He stood tall and proud, his olive-toned skin flawless, his physique proof of relentless dedication. His curly hair, tousled by a gentle breeze, framed a chiseled jawline that emphasized the quiet confidence in his gaze. And his eyes—reminiscent of honey in sunlight—spoke volumes without uttering a word.

Whew, this man is fine, she thought, her knees practically giving out. She felt like she might melt right there. But as good as he looked—and felt—standing so close, a quiet voice in her head reminded her to stay grounded.

I really need to be careful with this one, she thought.

The struggle between what she wanted and what she knew better was real. She'd been down that road before—getting too close too soon, only to end up hurt. Even her marriage had fallen apart when her ex turned out to be nothing like the man he pretended to be.

She knew this time she wouldn't let her body or her emotions take the lead. Her heart had gotten her in trouble before, but now, she was determined to let God guide her—not her feelings.

Lisa often wondered why God made it so difficult, knowing He designed people to love and crave each other. But this time around, she knew genuine friendship and truly getting to know someone were essential—because people could only pretend for so long.

Liam gently pulled away from a hug that felt almost too intimate. *Lord, have mercy—this man smells good,* she thought, glancing up at the ceiling with a silent plea: *Help me, Lord.* He helped her slip into her coat, his soft touch on her shoulders grounding her just enough to catch her breath. Then, with his hand outstretched, he asked, "May I hold your hand?"

You can hold way more than that, she realized.

Oh Lord, You're going to have to help me with these thoughts, this man knows how to treat a woman. Lisa's heart pounded as she slipped her fingers into his—a small, hopeful spark flickering inside her. *God, I hope Liam can't read my face right now,* she thought, forcing a smile as she lowered her eyes to regain composure.

As Liam walked her to his two-door Bentley coupe, a warm feeling settled over her from the simple act of holding his hand. Inside his spotless car, she remembered her father's advice: *Pay attention to how a man treats his things—it might tell you how he'll treat you.*

Yet memories of her failed marriage—how her ex's neat, polished ways had masked a lack of real love—reminded her to tread carefully. As she settled into the plush leather seat beside Liam, she couldn't help but wonder if history might repeat itself.

They set off on a short drive, exchanging light conversation as the city's bustle gave way to open roads. When the faint tang of salty air drifted through the vents, Lisa suspected they were heading for the beach—and as they rounded the final corner, her guess was confirmed. A sweeping stretch of coastline lay before them, breathtaking and seemingly endless. To her surprise, this was their destination.

Though the setting was undeniably romantic, Lisa couldn't help feeling slightly overdressed in her black lace dress and favorite red pumps—but she resolved to make it work. When Liam came around to open her door, she stepped out and paused to admire the ocean—the crash of the waves both exhilarating and humbling.

"Wow, just beautiful," she murmured, still taking in the view when Liam knelt down and gently patted his knee. "Put your foot here," he suggested, reaching into a small tote bag. From within, he produced a pair of gold flip-flops adorned with rhinestone bows.

As he slipped them onto her feet, the gesture felt surprisingly intimate. Even on one knee, his face came close enough for her to feel the warmth of his breath as he carefully removed her pumps. Lisa's heart raced, a shiver running down her spine at the brush of his fingers. *These broad shoulders and muscular arms,* she thought, trying not to stare. *And these lips? Have mercy!*

"There, I knew it would fit."

Thankful she'd just gotten a pedicure, Lisa appreciated his thoughtful care. She took his hand without hesitation, savoring the moment and feeling grateful for his kindness.

They strolled along the beach, the cool breeze ruffling her hair and filling her with anticipation. She couldn't help but smile at Liam's choice to start the evening with a quiet coastal walk—it was simple, thoughtful, and unexpectedly perfect.

"Look at that beautiful yacht," Lisa pointed out. "I've never seen one so beautiful," she added, half hoping to deflect her own overwhelming feelings, even as her gut told her Liam knew just how taken she was.

Liam's eyes lit up with a knowing smile as he followed her gaze. With a gentle tug on her hand, he urged her onward, his quiet confidence palpable as they approached the yacht—now only about 10 yards away.

"Have you ever been on a yacht, Ms. Franklin?" he asked.

"I've been on big yachts at client parties, but never a sleek private one like this. She's a real beauty, isn't she?" Lisa said, admiring the vessel as it bobbed against the water. When she turned to gauge his reaction, her heart fluttered—Liam was looking directly into her eyes.

"I think she's absolutely breathtaking," he said, his grin melting away any lingering doubts.

Determined to show him she wasn't simply swayed by appearances, Lisa teased playfully, "You're laying it on pretty thick, Mr. Grayson."

"I don't take your yes lightly, Ms. Franklin. I consider myself very privileged that you agreed to spend Valentine's Day with me," Liam replied earnestly.

As they continued walking, Lisa appreciated the silence Liam allowed to fall between them—a peaceful space as the sun hovered low on the horizon, not quite set but casting everything in gold. After a few moments, she broke the stillness, her voice soft but brimming with excitement. "Oh look, the yacht is docked now."

As they approached, a man on deck dressed like a butler greeted them warmly. "Mr. Grayson, this must be the lovely Ms. Franklin."

Lisa's eyes widened in astonishment as she slowly turned to look at Liam. "This yacht is for us?"

Pulling her arm forward, Liam led her up the ramp with a smile. Tears welled in Lisa's eyes as she realized

once again that Liam had done something no one else
ever had. It wasn't just the grand gesture—it was the
heartfelt care behind it. Stepping onto the deck, a wave
of gratitude washed over her.

The night unfolded with a magical sunset, romantic
music, and mouthwatering cuisine. Later, they stood on
the yacht's deck, watching fireworks burst in the sky—an
unexpected show that could be seen from the nearby
Disneyland, lighting up the night.

Beneath the dazzling burst of fireworks, their lips met
in a kiss that felt both electric and inevitable—charged
with all the longing and tension that had built throughout the evening. As their bodies drew close, it was as
if their souls found rhythm in the same breath. Lisa
felt weightless, caught in a rush of warmth and wonder.
Liam's lips, soft and sure, sparked something deep within
her—a quiet, unmistakable feeling that this just might be
love.

As the night drew to a close and Liam drove her home,
Lisa felt a twinge of nerves, wondering if he'd ask to come
inside. She had already decided she would say no—but
part of her couldn't help anticipating a goodnight kiss.

Instead, at her doorstep, he leaned in and gently kissed her forehead. The unexpected tenderness stirred something deeper than she expected, catching her completely off guard. Then, with a soft smile, he handed her a handwritten letter.

With trembling hands, she accepted it, a rush of emotion flooding her senses. He walked her to the door, thanked her for the evening, and waited quietly as she unlocked it.

Only after she stepped inside and turned to give him a final smile did he head back to his car. Lisa stood just beyond the door, heart full, watching until his taillights disappeared down the street.

In that moment, she knew without a doubt—she had found someone truly special. A man who wasn't just pursuing her, but cherishing her.

"Did I just go on a date with Liam Grayson?" she mused, smiling with a twinkle in her eye as she caught her reflection in the mirror by the door.

Instead of calling her girlfriend Nanji to recount every detail, Lisa chose to savor the moment—basking in the rare gift of feeling truly seen. With trembling fingers, she unfolded the letter to reveal Liam's handwritten words:

"Thank you for an unforgettable evening, Lisa. Your laughter, your grace, and your kindness lit up my world tonight. I hope this is only the beginning of something beautiful."

A rush of emotion swept over her as she read his message—each word a tender promise, capturing the magic of the night on paper. More than any grand gesture, what touched her most was the handwritten note—a sincere expression of affection that no text message could ever match.

Yet even in the glow of it all, a quiet caution lingered in the back of her mind. Liam was steadily winning her heart, but Lisa knew too well the pain of trusting too quickly.

Later that night, alone in the stillness of her room, she opened her journal and, with trembling hands, began to pray.

"Lord, thank You for the unexpected joy Liam has brought into my life. Help me not to rush headlong into the unknown or let the intoxication of romance cloud my judgment. Grant me the wisdom to discern Your will in every step I take."

Tears welled in her eyes as each word became a fragile offering of trust—a quiet plea for God to protect her heart from disappointment.

As she closed her journal, a peaceful reassurance washed over her. Her resolve was renewed. Her heart was no longer just her own—it was entrusted to the One who held it, confident that He would guide her safely through the stormy seas of love to lasting joy.

CHAPTER TWENTY-FOUR

THE FRANKLIN MEN

THE FISHING TRIP

E arly in the morning, as soft light crept through the windows, Henry lingered at the edge of the kitchen doorway. In the gentle hum of activity, he watched Lila and Jordan preparing for the day's fishing trip—a time-honored ritual that had brought the Franklin men together for as long as he could remember.

He observed Jordan meticulously arranging the sodas on the counter, ensuring that no one would go thirsty on their expedition. Nearby, Lila moved with practiced care, directing Jordan to the pantry where neat rows of water awaited and calmly counting out the lunches. Each sandwich and snack was prepared with love, and Henry noted with quiet pride how every meal bore the names of the men in the family—Henry, Sam, Bo, Angel, and Josh.

A soft smile played on his lips as he acknowledged that these humble preparations were not only fueling a day of adventure—they were nurturing the very heart of a deep family tradition.

As the Franklin men began gathering in the kitchen, Henry leaned against the doorway and watched the scene unfold with quiet satisfaction. He noticed how Lila's eyes sparkled with maternal pride as she looked upon her sons and grandsons—the very embodiment of her lifelong labor and love.

He heard Bo's sincere, "You're the best, Mom," echo softly in the background—a simple phrase that made Lila's eyes glisten. Henry recognized that for her, these homemade meals were far more than food; they were heartfelt tokens of all she had poured into raising them.

After gathering their homemade lunches and exchanging heartfelt goodbyes in the kitchen, the Franklin men piled into Bo's sleek new Denali. The atmosphere inside the car was charged, hinting that the journey ahead was as significant as the destination. With a practiced motion, Sam reached out to silence the music.

"So how's the single life, Bo?" he asked.

Sam's inquiry was casual yet tinged with genuine curiosity—a subtle attempt to forge a deeper connection with his brother. However, Bo responded with a roll of his eyes, a defense mechanism masking his vulnerability.

Angel's infectious laughter filled the cabin, his enthusiasm breaking through any lingering tension.

"Yeah, I can't wait to hear this," young Josh chimed in playfully, adding his own brand of humor to the question.

Amidst all the light-hearted teasing, Henry observed with a fond smile, his heart quietly swelling with pride as he took in the genuine joy shared between his sons and grandsons.

"What single life? Trinity is still my girl," Bo retorted, shrugging off the probing question with a trace of annoyance.

"Uhm, Dad, you and Mom have been divorced for a good six months now," Josh interjected, his voice thick with confusion.

Sam quickly added, "Oh, I see somebody hasn't accepted it yet."

Despite the teasing, Bo remained unyielding. His voice was filled with rock-solid determination as he declared that Trinity was still the woman of his dreams. Even facing the reality of their divorce, he clung to hope and outlined his plan to win her back. At that moment, Henry interjected, his tone heavy with the weight of experience.

"Let it breathe, son."

"What does that mean, Pops?" Angel asked, his eyes lighting up as he sought further guidance.

Henry offered a gentle explanation, drawing on examples of athletes he knew Angel would understand. "Sometimes you have to pause to catch your breath after a rough quarter."

Henry emphasized that patience and reflection were necessary to truly understand the events that led to life's tough breaks—even a divorce. His words carried a quiet wisdom as he reminded them of the importance of allowing emotion and time to work their magic.

"Agreed," Josh chimed in, nodding in tandem with his grandfather's perspective. "I keep telling Dad to chill out," he added, glancing toward Bo with exasperation.

Sam, ever the observant one, noted Bo's stubborn persistence in searching for solutions. "I see you're not listening—so what's the plan?" he asked, genuinely curious about his brother's next steps.

Henry listened as Bo launched into his strategy, explaining how he planned to do the small, thoughtful things—arranging Trinity's favorite takeout, and he even signed up for a flower delivery subscription—to show her that he still cared.

In Henry's quiet mind, he noted that Bo's plan was simple yet stubborn, a desperate attempt to reignite the spark that once bound them together. Before long, Bo's voice cut through the conversation. "So, what's up with your marriage, Sam, since you're all up in mine?" he challenged, his tone laced with a hint of defensiveness.

Henry watched as Sam paused, his calm demeanor a stark contrast to Bo's fervor. "You're not married, Bo. You and Trinity are divorced," Sam clarified firmly, urging his brother to face reality.

A bittersweet pang washed over Henry as he absorbed the exchange. He had seen this pattern play out too many times—hopeful dreams clashing with harsh truths that sometimes acceptance of reality is the only way forward.

Henry leaned back in his seat as Sam began recounting how, despite initial reluctance, he and Paula were taking time to rediscover themselves. From Henry's vantage point, it was clear that Paula—once entirely devoted to the family—was now exploring her own passions, filling the empty house with new energy and interests.

Sam admitted, with a hint of surprise, that he, too, had found himself following suit. He had rekindled his long-lost passion for photography, spending hours capturing moments at parks and museums, even enrolling in an online class to sharpen his craft.

Henry listened with a mixture of pride and wistfulness as Angel then chimed in. Ever the advocate for independence, he insisted that a good relationship wasn't about clinging to one another but about bringing one's own life to the table.

His words, earnest and laced with pride, underscored a sentiment Henry had long held: that true growth often comes when both sides learn to stand on their own. As the playful banter carried on in the car, Henry listened with a mixture of amusement and quiet pride. He watched as Angel, his voice light with excitement, piped up.

"Actually, one of the inspectors the City sent out to my new carwash site was a real knockout, and I asked her out."

Henry couldn't help but smile as young Josh enthusiastically high-fived Angel and then blurted out, "Rate her on a scale of 1 to 10!"

Before Angel could reply, Sam—always quick to keep things in check—stepped in, cautioning them against objectifying women with such casual remarks. Despite the interruption, Angel's face broke into a mischievous grin as he quipped, "A strong 9," punctuating his answer with a playful wink toward his little cousin, Josh.

Laughter rippled through the car at the exchange, and Henry savored each chuckle, reminded of the youthful energy that once filled his youth. As he glanced at his son Sam, he admired the maturity with which Sam and Paula were navigating the empty-nester transition. Then, turning his attentive gaze to his grandson Angel, Henry couldn't resist injecting a bit of his own seasoned humor.

"So, how do you plan to sweep this strong 9 off her feet on your first date?" he asked, a twinkle of mischief lighting his eyes as he probed gently.

Angel's response came quickly—a straightforward suggestion of a classic dinner and a movie. However, his simple answer drew laughter from Henry, Sam, and Bo, who teasingly dismissed it as lacking any real spark.

Not to be outdone, young Josh seized the opportunity to showcase his budding ideas. With a confidence that belied his age, he outlined a grander plan: a cooking class followed by a romantic carriage ride under the stars, and capped off with a Broadway-style theater show. Angel raised an eyebrow at Josh's elaborate scheme.

"Oh really? And what makes your idea so special?" he challenged.

With a grin, Josh explained the thought and effort behind his plan, emphasizing how memorable experiences were crafted through grand gestures. As the men nodded, Henry agreed that the first date should leave the deepest impression.

Henry watched as youthful impatience bubbled up in the car. Young Josh shifted in his seat and, unable to contain his restlessness, called out, "How much longer?"

His eyes scanned the passing scenery with anxious curiosity. Bo shot a quick glance at the GPS before replying calmly, "We're about 15 minutes away from the fishing camp."

Bo launched into a vivid account of the strange dream he'd had the night before. Henry listened intently as Bo described a young boy walking alongside a bustling construction site, the rhythmic clang of machinery echoing in his ears.

Suddenly, according to Bo, a trumpeting sound cut through the noise, drawing the boy's attention—and that of a few startled onlookers—to a crazy sight: an elephant, massive and out of place against the urban backdrop.

Bo's narration grew urgent as he recounted how the elephant, ensnared by one of its ears, struggled against an unseen obstacle keeping it captive in the construction site.

As if the scene weren't surreal enough, Bo described how the distressed elephant transformed before his eyes into a baby elephant riding a bicycle accompanied by its mother.

A reflective silence descended over the car as Bo finished his retelling, and Henry's mind raced with the symbolism behind the dream. Clearing the quiet, Henry spoke with steady authority:

"The elephant represents you, Bo." His voice carried the gravity of many years of experience. "And the struggles you're facing—those challenges you're still contemplating—they're symbolized by that very mammal. Just as it wrestled with its restraint, you're locked in a battle with your own heart." Henry paused, his eyes softening as he surveyed his family in the car.

"And the young boy watching? He represents your son—a witness to the example you set, learning how to navigate life by watching you."

Henry also interpreted the construction site in the dream as a metaphor for the time and effort it takes to rebuild something that has been broken or lost.

Still, one element remained elusive. "As for the elephant transforming into the baby, I can't say for certain what that means," he admitted.

"But I sense if you share this dream with your mother, she might shed some light on that. Perhaps she holds the key to that mystery."

Henry's measured words hung in the air, and he could sense that his insights were resonating with the men. He noted the mix of awe and understanding that had passed between them when their collective burdens aligned.

Before the intensity of the discussion could overwhelm Bo, the car's GPS announced, "You've arrived."

After parking their car at the front, where their fishing boat was already docked, the Franklin men stepped out with purpose. They grabbed their lunches and fishing poles and moved steadily toward the vessel.

Gathering near the water's edge—with their laughter mingling with the crisp morning air and the boat gently bobbing at the dock—Henry stepped forward, ready to embrace another chapter of cherished tradition. He was convinced that their shared struggles would see them through whatever challenges.

Chapter Twenty-Five

ANGELA

A Flickering Flame

As Dr. Darren lent a hand to the movers, assisting with the final pieces of Angela's belongings, she couldn't help but feel a surge of gratitude. After months of staying with him and Melissa several nights a week—while still holding on to her old apartment—Angela was finally embracing the fresh start her uncle Bo had encouraged.

At his urging, she had upgraded to a larger apartment with a spare bedroom, a space that felt more grown-up and full of possibility. Bo had believed a change of environment might help her reset—not just her surroundings, but her mindset too.

Now, as she watched her things being carried inside, Angela felt a new kind of independence settling in. With each box unpacked and each piece of furniture arranged, her new apartment began to feel like more than just a place to live. It felt like a reset button. A new chapter. And as she looked around, surrounded by familiar comforts in an unfamiliar space, she knew—this was a beginning she needed.

The aroma of freshly delivered pizza filled the air as the refrigerator hummed softly in the background. A distant car horn blared, and the floor creaked beneath Dr. Darren's weight as he settled beside Angela.

She took a bite, glancing at him as he shifted the conversation toward her clinical responsibilities. His tone was calm, steady—mentoring, as always. Angela listened as he spoke about the importance of taking patient histories.

To her, it was more than a lesson; it was a reminder of how serious this path was. The way Dr. Darren explained things made it clear—every word from a patient mattered.

She noticed how he always circled back to the same core principles: thoroughness, attention to detail, the weight of listening. His belief in a careful, comprehensive approach to care stayed with her, each word reinforcing just how much was at stake in every diagnosis.

While indulging in pizza and professional discourse, Angela decided to flip the script. With a playful tilt of her head, she adopted the demeanor of a clinician, turning her full attention to Dr. Darren.

"So, tell me," she said, her voice laced with curiosity and something a little bolder, "any preexisting conditions I should know about?"

A mischievous glint danced in her eyes, but the question hung between them with weight far heavier than its surface suggested. The simmer that had lingered for months now crackled just beneath her skin.

As she continued, her tone dripped with flirtation, each word measured but daring. Her gaze lingered—on his lips, on his hands—pausing in ways that said more than her questions ever could.

Dr. Darren chuckled, but his eyes held something deeper, a spark that mirrored hers. The space between them felt charged, as if the walls themselves were holding their breath. She could feel the shift—this wasn't just banter anymore. It was an invitation.

With each question she tossed his way, Angela's pulse quickened, her heart drumming to a rhythm that matched the slow, steady rise of tension in the room.

The professional facade they'd maintained for months felt thinner now, fragile beneath the weight of glances that lingered too long and silences that said too much.

There had always been chemistry—an invisible current humming between them—but tonight, it was undeniable.

As their laughter echoed between bites of pizza, Angela found herself watching him more closely. The curve of his smile. The quiet warmth in his eyes. The way his leg brushed hers under the table and didn't move away.

She felt the questions bubbling inside her—not the clinical ones, but the dangerous ones.

Was he feeling this too?

Was it all in her head, or had something shifted?

There was a flicker behind Dr. Darren's eyes. His usual composure seemed shaken, and she caught the way his fingers tapped once against the table before he stilled them.

It was as if he were caught between two choices, and she was the weight tipping the scale. They were playing with fire. She knew it. She could feel it in the way the air crackled between them, in the way his gaze lingered a beat too long. The room felt dimmer somehow, shadows stretching along the walls like temptation itself was dancing just out of reach.

And still, she couldn't look away. It was like being pulled into an ocean current she couldn't fight. The tension had grown thick and suffocating, and her own body betrayed her—leaning slightly closer, matching his heat with her own.

A voice inside her screamed to stop, but she barely heard it. Then, with a slow, almost deliberate calm, Dr. Darren looked at her and asked,

"Now, how would you begin the physical exam?"

He asked the question with a calm she knew was anything but. His curiosity was laced with something heavier—something warmer—and Angela could feel the humidity in the air.

Her response was quick, direct, and just a little dangerous. Mischief curved her lips as she leaned into the moment.

"Do you want the textbook version, Dr. Darren," she began, her eyes sparkling, "or would you prefer a more... hands-on approach?"

Her words hung in the air, deliberate and charged. She watched his reaction closely—the way his shoulders shifted ever so slightly, the flicker of surprise that crossed his face. His smile didn't come all at once—it built, like something cracking open.

She recognized it. She'd seen flickers of it before. But now, alone in this apartment, with no one left to interrupt, it felt different. Real. Dangerous. A slow smile played across her own lips.

Tension hung thick in the air, heavy and charged. Angela watched as Dr. Darren's gaze dropped to her lips, then slowly returned to her eyes. He didn't say a word, but something passed between them—a question unspoken, an answer waiting in the silence.

"Why not, Dr. Angela? I'd love to be your model."

The words sent a jolt straight through her. His tone was teasing, but his eyes—those eyes—told her he wasn't just playing along. He was accepting the invitation.

"Okay, Mr. Darren," she replied, rising with a deliberate slowness that matched the mood. She pulled a chair out and gestured toward it, her tone light but her pulse hammering.

"If you could sit here, I'll check your vitals."

He obeyed without hesitation, his knees brushing against hers as he sat. He didn't move them. Neither did she. Angela cleared her throat softly, trying to keep her voice even.

"First, I'm going to observe the rise and fall of your chest."

Her gaze tracked the subtle motion of his breathing, and she had to resist the urge to press her hand against his chest, just to feel the rhythm for herself. She pretended to count under her breath, but her own heart was racing. He was watching her—she could feel it. His attention clung to her like heat on skin, and it only made it harder to concentrate.

"Now... I seem to be missing my pulse monitor," she said, her voice softer now. "Do I have permission to touch your wrist and take your pulse, Mr. Darren?"

He gave a slight nod, lips curving into a smile that made her stomach flip. Angela reached for his wrist, careful and controlled, though the moment her fingers made contact, she felt it—a jolt, a current that shot straight up her arm.

His pulse was racing. So was hers.

"Hmm," she murmured, a playful lilt in her tone.

"Your pulse is a little elevated." She let her gaze lift back to his.

"Are you nervous about anything?"

He didn't answer right away. Just held her stare. His smile deepened, slow and deliberate.

"Nervous isn't quite the word I'd use," he said, his voice low and thick with meaning. The effect of his words rippled through her like electricity. She felt it in her chest, in her fingertips, in the back of her neck.

Her confidence rose to meet it. His desire was no longer a secret—it was alive, undeniable, and aimed at her. Angela stepped closer, close enough to feel his breath, close enough that there was no turning back.

Her morals, her upbringing, the warnings in the back of her mind—all of it blurred under the weight of what she wanted. Right now, it was him. With a hand on his arm, she pulled him to his feet. Their bodies brushed, inches apart, breath to breath.

The clarity of it—*he wants me*—cut through every warning in her mind. The voice of reason tried to rise again, but she buried it beneath the thrill of his nearness. She knew the risk. She knew the rules. But right now, the only thing she could feel was the heat.

She paused, letting the moment hang, letting the tension stretch taut between them.

"How do you propose I take your temperature?"

Angela barely had time to draw breath before he moved. His hand slid to her face, fingers firm but trembling just slightly. The hunger in his eyes left no doubt.

And then he kissed her.

The contact sparked something explosive. His lips met hers with a hunger that matched her own, and Angela melted into it, her breath caught somewhere in her chest. She felt herself falling—into him, into the moment, into the delicious madness they'd been circling for months.

"Like this," she heard him whisper against her mouth, but the words were a blur. All she could focus on was the feel of him—warm, urgent, real.

Their kiss deepened, mouths colliding with a force that betrayed every bit of discipline they were trying to ignore.

Angela clutched his shirt, pulling him closer, no longer pretending she had control.

Her hair slipped from its clip. His hands found her waist, her back. Time dissolved. Clothes were forgotten, scattered. Her skin burned under his touch, and all that existed was this heat, this hunger, this reckless surrender.

She knew exactly what this was—what it meant, what it would cost—but as their bodies tangled in the dim light of her apartment, she couldn't stop. Didn't want to. For a moment, there was no past. No marriage. No title of mentor or mentee. Only two people on fire.

But as the flames of passion subsided, guilt came crashing in. The heat between them faded, replaced by a heavy, aching silence. Her apartment felt different now—like the room itself was recoiling from what had just happened.

Angela lay motionless, her skin still warm, but her spirit chilled with realization. She turned her head just in time to see Dr. Darren pulling on his jacket, his back already halfway to the door.

He didn't speak. Not even a glance.

The door opened. Closed. Gone.

She sat up slowly, pulling her knees to her chest. Her breathing was shaky. Her body still remembered every touch, every kiss—but her heart felt only the weight of betrayal.

Uncle Bo trusted him. The thought pierced her. Sharp. Shameful. It wasn't just Darren's marriage. It was her uncle's name, his friendship, his favor. He had opened a door to help her, and she'd walked right into fire.

"What did I just do?"

She buried her face in her hands. Uncle Bo had kept her secret. Covered for her. Gave her money to get into her new apartment. Called in favors. She had repaid him with betrayal.

The sharp ring of her phone cut through the silence like a slap. Angela flinched, her breath catching as she reached for it with trembling hands. The name on the screen stopped her cold.

Uncle Bo.

Her stomach turned. A chill slid down her spine. Of all people, why him? She stared at the screen as it lit up again, glowing like a judgment she couldn't outrun.

She let it ring.

Then again.

What if he hears it in my voice?

What if he asks about Dr. Darren?

The thought made her chest tighten.

If I don't answer, he'll know something's off, she told herself. *He always knows.* Her thumb hovered over the red decline button, but something deeper pushed her hand away.

Angela pressed the phone to her ear, heart pounding.

"Hey, baby girl," Bo's familiar voice rumbled gently. "Just checking on you. Everything okay with the new place?"

She swallowed hard. Her throat burned.

No, she wanted to say. *Everything's not okay.*

But she couldn't. Not after what she'd done. Not to him. So instead, she did the only thing she could do—she lied.

"Yeah," she whispered. "Just getting settled."

Bo said something else—something kind—but she barely heard it. Her heart was pounding, her skin hot with shame.

As the call ended, the silence wrapped around her like a verdict. She sat there, phone still in hand, breath shallow.

Then it came.

A burst of laughter outside—low, distant, but unmis-takably male.

Angela jumped.

It wasn't Darren.

It wasn't anyone she recognized. But in that moment, it sounded like the devil himself, mocking what she had just done. She closed her eyes, the sound echoing in her mind long after it faded—a reminder that some fires don't just burn. They follow you.

Chapter Twenty-Six

SELENA

When It Rains Inside

The soft flicker of candlelight danced across the white tablecloth, casting muted gold against Selena's face as she sat quietly at the corner table. The restaurant was elegant, its ambiance curated to impress—dim lighting, hushed tones, and polished silverware that sparkled like promise. But to Selena, it all felt like a charade. Luxury didn't mask pain.

She traced slow circles on her purse with a trembling finger—not to fidget, but to feel something she could control. The scent of rosemary and seared meat wafted from the kitchen, but her stomach turned instead of growling. Her tired eyes, outlined in carefully applied makeup, couldn't hide the hollowness that sleepless nights had carved into them.

A faint purple bloom peeked from beneath her blouse sleeve—barely visible, but present. A bruise from Richard. A *"playful"* pinch, he said. Selena stared at it blankly, as if the shadow under her skin held the answer to a question she no longer dared ask.

It had been two and a half months since Jordan left to live with her grandparents. Two and a half months of deafening silence at home. The once lively house now echoed with every footstep.

Sometimes, Selena would pause by Jordan's room, letting the quietness crush her before moving on. How had she ended up here—fighting to feel like a mother, a wife, a whole person?

He hadn't hit her again—not in the way people defined it. But he'd started playfully pinching her. They were light enough to be dismissed, yet deep enough to leave a mark. What had initially seemed harmless now became the norm, blurring the lines between affection and aggression.

And then there were the unannounced school visits that had become a recurring source of discomfort for Jordan. She said the visits felt performative. Jordan said what made them even more awkward was that Richard barely spoke. He stared. Nodded. Occasionally handed her cash. But there was no warmth, no engagement.

And worst of all, Selena had lied for him. When her mother Lila demanded answers after Richard popped up again without warning, Selena claimed she knew. Claimed she forgot to tell Jordan.

Why had she done that? Maybe it was the way her mother's voice rose, slicing through her nerves. Maybe she was trying to shield Richard. *But from what?*

A familiar cologne broke her thoughts. Richard entered the restaurant, his posture rigid, jaw tight. He spotted her and offered a tight-lipped smile that never reached his eyes. Selena's breath caught when she noticed the flick of his gaze toward a young woman at the bar. Her stomach churned—not in jealousy, but in recognition. It was a pattern, and she hated it.

It was as if he liked to stare down other women in her presence. She'd catch him glancing from the corner of his eye, making sure she noticed. As if he took pleasure in making her feel insecure.

In the past, when she'd confront him about it, he'd gaslight her—ask what she was talking about, act like she was overreacting, jealous, imagining things. Today, she was here to talk to him about Jordan and didn't have the energy to address his stupid antics.

"I've got about 35 minutes," he stated sharply as he reached the table, glancing at his watch. No *hello*. No *how are you*. Just time limits and clipped tones.

As the server appeared to confirm their drink orders, Selena felt Richard's energy shift—like he couldn't wait for this to be over. The clink of glasses and soft piano in the background felt like cruel irony. Her heartbeat slowed in sync with her disappointment, as Richard's laugh reeked of mockery.

"You've got that look again. What? Think I was checking someone out? All in your imagination, Selena."

Selena looked at him. *Really* looked. His face still bore the charm that once wooed her, but now it masked something hollow.

"What are you talking about?" she said calmly, unwilling to take the bait.

Silence fell, thick as fog. Their order was taken—Richard barely glanced at the server—and Selena watched the interaction with growing shame. He was rude. Dismissive. Entitled. She felt heat rise to her cheeks. Not from embarrassment. From anger.

Why am I still here? She had spent 14 years enduring this. The bruises always faded, but the damage hadn't.*Is a two-parent household really worth this?* Jordan had left. And maybe... maybe it was time she did too.

"So?" Richard said, leaning back in his chair. "What's this lunch about? Every time you say we need to 'talk'"—he added air quotes—"it's never good."

Selena inhaled sharply. Her voice came steady, but her heart trembled. "It's about you showing up at Jordan's school unannounced."

She explained how uncomfortable it made their daughter. How Jordan felt the conversations were dry, forced. How it didn't feel fatherly—it felt staged. Selena didn't accuse. She simply relayed. Jordan wanted Sunday dinners, not surprise visits.

Richard scoffed. "So what? She doesn't want to see me, that's what I'm hearing. That doesn't matter—I'm her father."

Selena's spine straightened. "It does matter. She's not just some pawn you can drop in on for your ego. She has feelings."

"And yet," Richard said with a smirk, "she takes the money. Funny how she's uncomfortable but not enough to give that up."

His words landed like slaps. Selena blinked hard, trying to contain the swell of rage inside her. He wasn't listening. Not to her. Not to Jordan.

He kept going. Blamed her for the Christmas incident. Said Jordan would still be home if Selena hadn't "made a scene." Then he criticized her for confiding in her mother. Called it betrayal. Even questioned her faith.

In a final blow, he brought religion into the argument, reminding Selena of her Christian beliefs and how the Bible instructs wives to cleave to their husbands.

"That's not what that scripture means."

Selena snapped, cutting him off. "It says a man shall leave his parents and cleave to his wife. Not that a woman should cleave to a man who breaks her down."

Her voice trembled but didn't break.

"You've isolated me from everyone. Family members, college friends. I covered up your bruises. Remember the black eye? I had to use makeup just to look normal in public."

She leaned forward, voice low but cutting. "You say you're a father. So act like it. Respect your daughter. Stop using money as a band-aid for your absence."

Richard didn't respond. He stood abruptly, chair scraping against the floor, and left. Just like that. No apology. No rebuttal. Gone.

Selena sat frozen, staring through the restaurant window as his car peeled away. Her chest felt tight, but she didn't move. She barely registered the server arriving with their food, setting the dishes down gently, clearly embarrassed that a few nearby customers had witnessed what had just happened.

A moment later, an older waiter approached—a different one than before. He looked to be in his sixties, with silver hair neatly combed back and a posture that was proud yet gentle. He glanced at her face, then at the untouched food, and hesitated.

"Miss... may I?" he asked quietly, gesturing to the empty chair across from her. Selena nodded, too numb to speak. He sat down slowly, his hands resting calmly on the table between them.

"I've been working in this restaurant for a long time," he said, his voice low and steady. "And I can always tell when someone's pretending they're okay."

He didn't rush his words. There was no judgment in his tone—just presence. Just care.

"I don't know your story," he continued, "but I saw that man leave. The way he walked out... the way he spoke to you..." He paused, emotion briefly tightening his throat. "I have daughters. And if one of them was sitting here, I'd want someone to say something."

Selena's throat burned, her gaze fixed on the cloth napkin she had twisted into a rope in her lap.

"I watched you stand up for yourself," he said softly. "That's not weakness. That's strength. Real strength."

She blinked hard, and the first tear slipped free.

"How much harder do you want it to get, babygirl?"

He gave a slight nod toward the bar, and moments later, another server approached with a small to-go cup in hand. The older man took it gently and placed it in front of Selena.

"Here, sweetheart," he said with quiet care. "Chamomile. Helps when your soul's been rattled."

She reached for it, her fingers trembling. Soft and shaky, she held the cup close and met his eyes—just for a moment. Her gratitude ran too deep for words.

"Whatever comes next, just remember—peace is your birthright." He stood gently and reached for the plates.

"I'll box this up for you," he said with a nod, as if giving her permission to rest. Then he walked away—leaving her alone again, but no longer unseen.

The warmth of the tea in her palms didn't erase the ache in her chest, but it reminded her that kindness still existed. That she still deserved it.

"Peace is my birthright... wow."

Selena whispered the words, letting them settle into her spirit like a seed of hope.

When the older man returned, she thanked him with a trembling hand. As he set the neatly packed to-go boxes on the table, Selena instinctively reached for her purse.

He gently raised a hand. "Lunch is on us," he said with a kind smile. "You've had enough to carry today."

Her throat tightened. She managed a small nod, gratitude swelling in her chest.

With the boxes in hand, she exited the restaurant and walked slowly to the car. The wind had picked up slightly, brushing loose strands of hair across her cheek. She unlocked the door, slid into the driver's seat, and set the food beside her.

With hands resting on the steering wheel, she stared through the windshield—and as if on cue, it began to rain. Soft at first. Then steadier. As if the sky itself felt her pain and decided to weep with her.

For a moment, she just sat there.

The water streaked down the glass, blurring the world outside. But unlike her life, the windshield cleared with every sweep of the wipers. And something about that contrast broke her.

Then came the whisper—that still small voice of God that said, *"You don't have to live like this anymore."*

It was subtle. But sometimes, life shifts in the quiet. A holy kind of clarity that shows up when you need it most.

The tears came—quiet at first, then full. They didn't bring peace, but they brought release. Her body trembled with each breath, but something inside her had shifted. She didn't just feel ready to leave—this time, she was ready to move.

Selena picked up her phone and opened a message thread with her friend Shannon, a real estate agent who knew more about her situation than most.

"If you still have that house you told me about... I'm ready."

She stared at the screen for a long second, her heart pounding. Then she hit send. It wasn't dramatic. It wasn't loud. But it was real. It was forward.

And she knew—God saw that text, too.

He'd been ready to help her all along. He just needed her to take the first step. She couldn't stay in this cycle. Not for Jordan. Not for herself. She needed to be free.

Chapter Twenty-Seven

LISA

Floor Seats

A low hum of bass rolled through the concourse as Lisa stepped into the packed Lakers stadium, the electric charge in the air making the hairs on her arms stand at attention. As they passed, heads turned in admiration. Flashbulbs popped, and murmurs of "Wow, look at them" drifted through the air. Lisa straightened her shoulders, a wave of confident happiness washing over her, her sister-friend a comforting presence beside her.

Beneath it lay a thrill she'd never felt in all her years covering games. She was a sports reporter, but her usual press box perch was worlds away from this: no media risers, no official press seats. The seating attendant led them to true floor seats, the very same folding chairs league VIPs coveted, mere feet from the court.

They settled into their folding chairs. The cool metal frame pressed beneath her fingertips as she let the reality sink in – *I am sitting in the floor seats at a Lakers game*, she thought.

A gravelly voice boomed over the PA:

"Ladies and gentlemen, welcome to tonight's matchup. Ready for some pre-games?"

The crowd erupted, the sound ricocheting off the rafters in a roar that vibrated through Lisa's chest. She felt it in her bones—an excitement that mingled with a flutter of nerves as she scanned the names on the roster board. Nanji tapped her knee.

"It's been a full 30 days, and you still haven't filled me in on all the juicy details of you and Liam's Valentine's date. Spill the tea, honey!"

A ripple of laughter passed between them. Lisa's cheeks

warmed. *Why do I still get so shy talking about him?* She tucked a loose strand of hair behind her ear and remembered how her skin tingled when Liam's hand gently slipped off her heels and eased her into the soft flip-flops he'd bought—sending shivers down her spine.

"He rented a yacht," she blurted, surprised by her own boldness. She leaned in, voice dropping. Nanji whooped and slapped her thigh. The cushioned slap echoed in Lisa's ear like a drumbeat.

"I knew it! This guy's a keeper."

Like two high-school teenagers, Lisa eagerly shared all the juicy details with Nanji.

She recounted how Liam had thoughtfully bought her flip-flops so her feet wouldn't ache, the thrill of spotting the yacht, the surprise when she realized it was theirs alone, and the lavish dinner prepared by the chef. She painted the magical moment when fireworks lit up the sky, making the evening feel otherworldly.

"Okay, girl—did you two kiss or what?"

Nanji asked, playful grin in full effect. Lisa blushed but couldn't hide her smile as she admitted they had. Nanji celebrated with a high-five.

"I knew it. This guy is the one—I can feel it."

Lisa held up a hand. "Easy, girl. We're taking things slow."

After all, Nanji knew all about her ex-NBA player husband—how that marriage had ended in bitterness. That she'd even gone out with Liam at all felt like a miracle. Nanji launched into her case:

"Your ex, Mr. Entertainer-of-the-Year, lived for the spotlight. Loud, flamboyant, selfish, arrogant, too friendly with the ladies—you should never have married him." She paused for effect, then added,

"But Liam is quiet, understated, humble. He's famous but he's got no ego. He's a philanthropist, loves his family, and has no kids. Girl, they are night and day."

Lisa nodded. She'd been so nervous about seeing Liam again—scheduling a second date between their hectic lives had felt impossible. Yet here they were, talking every day, FaceTiming whenever they could, and he still sent her a gorgeous bouquet each week.

Their laughter faded as the announcer cut in, introducing the starting lineups. The atmosphere in the stadium became even louder as the music blared and the screams of fans of all ages filled the air, sharing in the excitement of the game starting.

Lisa felt butterflies in her stomach as she anticipated Liam's name being called. She eagerly searched the line-up, hoping to catch a glimpse of him on the court. The energy in the stadium was infectious, and Lisa couldn't help but get caught up in the thrill.

Players strode onto the court to boisterous applause, sneakers squeaking on hardwood like paintbrush strokes on canvas. Nanji was also keeping an eye out for Liam when she spotted him and nudged Lisa.

"Girl, he's looking at you!"

Turning her head, they locked eyes, and he winked at her. She caught her breath when she saw him—Liam's tall frame, his name stitched in bold letters across his jersey. Her heart melted at the gesture, but she decided to play it cool. She nodded and smiled with her eyes, acknowledging him discreetly.

Oh my God, did he really wink? Did he forget the cameras? she thought.

Throughout the game, Lisa and Nanji were a dynamic duo, cheering on the team with enthusiasm and sharing lighthearted banter. Nanji, always the energetic one, was jumping out of her seat with every basket, while Lisa, with her newfound appreciation for Liam, couldn't help but smile every time he touched the ball.

As the game progressed, Lisa couldn't deny the spark she felt whenever she caught Liam's eye. His energy, his easy confidence—it stirred something in her she hadn't felt in a long time.

Nanji, ever the supportive friend, didn't miss a thing. She caught the way Lisa's eyes lingered a little too long, the way her smile softened when Liam's name came up. With a playful nudge, Nanji grinned.

"You're falling for him, aren't you?"

Lisa laughed it off at first, but the way her heart stumbled in her chest told a different story. She wasn't sure if it was excitement or fear—but either way, Nanji's words hit closer to the truth than she wanted to admit.

The final buzzer resounded through the stadium, signaling Liam's team's victory. The crowd erupted into cheers, the air electric as purple, gold, and black confetti rained down onto the court.

Nanji nudged Lisa just as Liam began heading in their direction. Lisa's heart skipped a beat—he was walking toward her.

She blinked, stunned. Liam's bold move to approach her in front of everyone caught her completely off guard. She knew how the media worked—someone would be snapping photos, someone would be asking questions.

Nervously, Lisa turned to Nanji, who gave her a sly wink as she grabbed her purse.

"Gotta go, girl. This spotlight is all yours."
"Nanji, please don't leave me," Lisa whispered.

"You deserve this, Lisa. Act like it—and act like it now." And just like that, Nanji was gone, weaving toward the media section where several of their colleagues were already preparing to interview players.

Feeling the heat of Liam's body and the brush of his lips so tantalizingly close to her ear, Lisa quickly composed her face, keenly aware of the onlookers gawking at their interaction. Slightly out of breath, Liam leaned in, his voice low against her skin.

"I've got a few interviews," he whispered, "but meet me

outside the locker room area. Please."

Lisa exhaled, her heart pounding. She weaved her way backstage, showing her media badge and finding what she hoped would be a private, out-of-view spot near the locker rooms.

What are you doing, Lisa?
Are you really ready for this again?

And yet... here she was.

Drawn back into the orbit of someone who could shatter all the careful walls she had rebuilt. She closed her eyes for a moment, breathing in deeply.

When she opened her eyes, Liam was weaving his way toward her, his face lighting up the second he saw her. A smile tugged at her lips before she could stop it. He greeted her warmly, his easy smile disarming her.

"Congratulations on the win," she said, unable to hide the admiration in her voice. "You were amazing out there."

"Thanks," he replied, voice smooth and confident. "Just glad you were here to see it. Wanted to make sure the seat—and the view—didn't disappoint."

The flirty glint in his eyes made Lisa blush despite herself.

"Not at all. Thanks again for the sideline pass," she said, her gaze lingering on his. Any awkwardness between them melted as they fell into effortless conversation. Liam teased her about Nanji's animated cheers, and Lisa laughed, swatting at his arm.

"Nanji was practically coaching from the sideline," he said, grinning.

"What can I say? That's my girl," she replied, flashing a playful smile.

The chemistry between them was undeniable—easy, electric. Their eyes kept locking like they were both waiting for the other to say what they were really thinking.

"So... where'd Nanji run off to?" he asked.

"Post-game press conference. She left me to fend for myself," Lisa said, shaking her head fondly.

Their eyes met again—and held. The air seemed to thicken between them.

Without warning, Liam pulled her into a hug. Surprised, Lisa leaned in, heart pounding. Despite the game, he still smelled good—clean, warm, familiar.

"Didn't mean to catch you off guard," he murmured near her ear. "I haven't even showered... but I couldn't help myself."

Before Lisa could reply, his manager appeared, reminding him of his other media obligations. Liam sighed, clearly reluctant.

"I've gotta run. But... how about dinner in a couple hours?" His gaze dropped to her lips—and lingered.

Lisa smirked, tilting her head slightly. "A hug was one thing, Mr. Grayson," she warned softly. "But if you kiss me... we'll end up on TMZ."

Liam chuckled, a low, deep sound that sent a shiver down her spine. His eyes finally—reluctantly—found their way back to hers.

"I'll behave," he promised, flashing a grin that made her stomach flip.

"I'll be ready at eight," she said, her pulse quickening.

As he turned to leave, Lisa watched him go, a soft smile tugging at her lips.

Lord, have mercy... that man is fine, she thought, shaking her head slightly. Her nerves buzzed with anticipation.

Dinner with Liam sounded like the perfect end to an already unforgettable night.

Chapter Twenty-Eight

ANGELA

Tangled Loyalties

As Angela's eyes fluttered open, she found herself alone in the sunlit master bedroom of her new apartment. The warmth of the morning seeping through the curtains. With a heavy sigh, she sat up, her mind already consumed by the weight of her actions the night before. Guilt and shame gnawed at Angela's conscience as she replayed the events of the past few weeks in her mind with Dr. Darren.

Yet, each encounter seemed to blur the lines further, igniting a fire within her that she struggled to extinguish. Closing her eyes and taking a deep breath, the lingering scent of Darren's cologne still clung to walls in her bedroom. A brief sexy flashback coming to her, the way his touch sent shivers down her spine.

As Angela rose to stretch, she caught her reflection in the sliding mirrored doors of her closet. Turning away quickly, she found it increasingly difficult to face herself. Seeing her own image was jarring. She knew right from wrong, and looking at herself directly in the mirror felt like judgment. Having grown up in the church, Angela was well-versed in her Bible, and adultery ranked high among the sins.

Angela tried to rationalize her actions, attributing them to loneliness and the way Dr. Darren supported her. She had often heard that you can't help who you fall in love with and that love is love.

But is it? Would love betray Melissa's kindness taking her into their home? Would love break up someone's marriage? What was she thinking? Love? Did she love Darren, or did she just want Darren?

The questions swirled in her mind, each one adding to her confusion and guilt. Deep down, she knew what she felt for Darren was not love, at least not the kind of love that was true and selfless.

She remembered sitting in church hearing a guest speaker talking about sin and how it will take you farther than you want to go. That description was definitely the predicament she was in.

Her Dad would be ready to kill Darren. Her uncle would feel so betrayed. Her little cousins would be disappointed in her. The women in her family would think she was a slut. Melissa would be devastated.
But deep down, she liked it—craved it. They'd had three encounters so far, and the adrenaline rush of the forbidden was like a drug. Darren set her body on fire in ways she didn't even know. It was intoxicating—how he touched her, claimed her, made her feel not just wanted... but consumed.

On the flip sides, the guilt of betraying her own principles loomed large immediately afterwards. She noticed as well that Darren's visits were short and how he seemed rushed to get out of her place. With a heavy heart, Angela debated her next move.

Should she confront Dr. Darren and risk ruining their professional relationship? The thought of losing his mentorship stung, but the guilt of their secret encounters was a sharper pain.

Should she try to set boundaries, knowing deep down she might not be able to resist his charm? Perhaps, the only solution was to distance herself, to move away and start fresh.

The sound of a key turning in the lock jolted her out of her thoughts. It was too early for Darren, and there was only one other person with a spare key. Sending a surge of panic through her chest. The sharp sound of her mother's footsteps approached as the soft creak of the door opened.

"Mom, you scared me. What are you doing here?" Angel said jumping out of the bed, Paula stepped inside.

At first, seeing her mother brought a sense of comfort,

a familiar face, but Angela's initial relief quickly mor-
phed into growing apprehension. Paula's warm smile
and outstretched arms seemed like a lifeline in the chaos
of Angela's thoughts.

But beneath the surface, a knot of anxiety tightened in
Angela's stomach. Paula's surprise visit was unexpected,
and Angela couldn't shake the feeling that her mother's
timing was too perfect, almost too coincidental.

What if she sensed something was wrong? As Angela
and Paula made their way to the kitchen, she became
increasingly nervous.

"You know, Angela," Paula began, her voice gentle, "I was
thinking about your spare bedroom. It's just sitting there
empty. Have you thought about turning it into a small
home office?

Angela's heart skipped at the mention of the spare bedroom. That was where Darren had once shown up without a word, shut the door behind him, and led her into
the empty room. No small talk. No pretense. Just raw,

aching urgency as he had her right there on the bare carpet—like he couldn't wait another second.

"Uh, yeah, that's a good idea, Mom," Angela replied, forcing a smile. "I'll think about it."

"Are you okay, Angela?" Paula asked, her voice laced with worry.

"Yeah, Mom, I'm fine," Angela replied, her voice barely above a whisper. "Just tired, I guess."

But Paula wasn't convinced. She reached out, placing a comforting hand on Angela's shoulder. "You know you can talk to me about anything, right?" Paula said, her voice gentle but firm. "I'm here for you, no matter what."

Angela's eyes brimmed with tears as she met her mother's loving gaze. For a moment, she wanted nothing more than to let it all spill out—to confess everything. But the words lodged in her throat, choked by fear and thick with shame. So instead, she did what she always did. She forced a smile.

"I'm great Mom" Angela replied, her voice barely above a whisper.

Despite her inner turmoil, Angela tried her best to engage in the conversation, sharing snippets of her life while carefully dodging any mention of her mentors Darren and Melissa. Angela laughed at all the right moments, nodding along as her mother shared more details from her trip alone.

As Angela and Paula continued their conversation, a knock at the door jolted them. Angela's heart leaped into her throat as she exchanged a nervous glance towards the door. Paula popped up to answer it for her as Angela was still in her pajama's.

"Another Amazon package, girl you are just like your father" Paula stated jokingly.

Angela's mind raced with panicked thoughts, but before she could respond, the door swung open, revealing Dr. Darren standing on the threshold, a forced smile plastered across his face.

"Darren!" Paula exclaimed, her surprise evident in her voice. "What a pleasant surprise."

Angela's heart hammered against her ribs, a frantic drum solo threatening to burst through her chest.

"Hey, Paula, Angela," Darren greeted them, his voice strained as he stepped into the room. "I hope I'm not interrupting anything. I was just in the neighborhood and thought I'd stop by to say hello and see how our future doctor is doing."

Angela's heart sank at Darren's fabricated excuse, her hand instinctively flying to her messy bun. She exchanged a nervous glance towards her mother, her stomach churning as a million panicked thoughts raced through her mind.

"Darren, I haven't seen you since the Christmas party. How's Melissa?" Paula said, her tone light, looking past the door for Melissa.

Darren's smile faltered for a fraction of a second before he recovered, his eyes darting nervously meeting Angela's.

"Oh, you know Melissa never gets a free moment. I'm still on my sabbatical and thought I'd drop by to catch up," Darren replied, his voice strained.

Angela's heart leaped into her throat and her stomach churned at Darren's words, remembering their mock clinical and what it turned into. The air in the room thickened with each passing moment as Angela avoided eye contact.

"Isn't that nice, Angela?" Paula said, her voice cheerful but with a hint of skepticism.

"Oh I'm sorry, I didn't mean to be rude. Yes, how nice of you."

Angela forced a smile, her cheeks burning with embarrassment as she looked down tugging on the loose pajama bottoms that suddenly felt so flimsy.

"Oh I'm sorry. Please forgive me. I should have called first. Angela's been working so hard lately, I had to come by check in on her" Darren interjected, his voice dripping with false enthusiasm.

"I'm managing well" Angela said, her gaze a silent plea for some kind of miracle that would explain this unexpected visit. She wanted nothing more than to scream "get out of my house", but knew she couldn't, not with her mother standing right there.

"Actually, I only had a few minutes. I have a round of golf..." Darren's voice trailed, his eyes flickering nervously between Angela and Paula. With a forced chuckle, Darren excused himself and hurried out the door.
Paula's gaze lingered on Angela for a long beat, as she closed the door behind him. Angela forced a smile, her cheeks burning with a mixture of embarrassment and dread, struggling to find words, her mind racing with excuses and half-truths.

"That was nice of him," she said, pulling on the short

shorts of her pajamas as her heart sank.

In that all-knowing tone her mother had mastered since Angela was a child, Paula walked over, hand on her hip and shouted:

"Angela Nicole Franklin, what the hell is going on!"

Chapter Twenty-Nine

BO

A Fresh Start (or Maybe Not)

B o stood in front of the mirror, smoothing a fitted T-shirt over his torso, studying the way it hugged his arms and shoulders. *Not bad*, he thought with a smirk, flexing briefly and admiring the familiar lines of his muscles.

Today wasn't just about Josh's weekend visit—it was an opportunity. An opportunity to remind Trinity of the man he still was, and maybe, just maybe, spark a reminder of the man she'd met when they first fell in love.

He spritzed the air with a clean citrus scent, watching it drift through the morning sunlight slicing across the hardwood floors. The house smelled like fresh beginnings or at least he needed it to.

Bo queued up a mellow playlist on the Bose speakers, the low hum of bass warming the space around him. Earlier he'd vacuumed every inch of the living room, fluffed the throw pillows, even wiped down the counters twice. He wanted everything to be perfect. No, better than perfect.

At the foyer, he checked the picnic basket one more time: candles, Trinity's favorite author, chocolates, gourmet coffee, a mug he'd picked out just for her—the words "You Are Loved" etched across the side. His chest tightened a little. *This was more than a basket. This was a statement.*

The crunch of tires on gravel jolted him from his thoughts. Bo wiped his palms on his jeans and headed outside, forcing an easy smile across his face.

"Hey, Trinity, Josh," he called warmly, waving them up the walkway. "Come on in. I have something for you, Trinity," he added, lifting the basket slightly.

Josh shot him a look—a mixture of amusement and mortification. *Ease up, Dad,* it seemed to say. Bo ignored him. His focus was on Trinity. She stepped inside, her eyes scanning the house.

"Wow," she said, "the house looks really nice, Bo."

He felt a rush of pride.

Josh sniffed the air dramatically. "What's that smell, Mack Daddy?" he joked, raising his eyebrows. Bo laughed along with them, a warm, fleeting moment he clung to.

This was what he missed. Family. Laughter. Belonging. With a flick of his wrist, Bo presented the basket, trying not to look too eager. "Here, Trinity. This is for you."

Josh groaned under his breath.

"Uh, bye Mom. I'm out." He bolted upstairs, muttering *"Too soon,"* loud enough for Bo to hear. Bo smothered a sigh. *That boy,* he thought, half exasperated, half amused. Still, he couldn't help feeling the sting of Josh's reaction. Taking a breath, Bo turned back to Trinity, his pulse hammering a little too hard.

"I just want you to enjoy your weekend," he said, voice earnest. "I hope this helps." For a second—just a second—he thought he saw her soften.

"Thank you, Bo," she said politely, her smile kind but guarded. "It's very thoughtful, I'm late for an appointment". And just like that, she was gone—leaving him standing there, a goodbye barely brushing the air between them.

Bo forced a grin as Josh wandered back into view, shaking his head.

"A picnic basket?" Josh teased, incredulous.

Bo chuckled, masking the pang of disappointment tightening in his chest. "Yeah, you don't know nothing about that," he said lightly. "You ready to go to your grandparents'?"

Josh grinned, loosening up. "Yeah, let's go."

They headed outside together, the afternoon sun bright and a little too hot. Josh threw one last jab over his shoulder. "Did you pick up the house in that tight muscle shirt?"

Bo laughed, a low rumble. "Just trying to look presentable," he shrugged. "Gotta make a good impression."

"Sure, Dad," Josh teased, climbing into the car. "Whatever you say."

Bo tossed him the keys. "Your permit is about to expire. Time to get that license."

Josh's face lit up. "For real? You're letting me drive?"

Bo leaned back in the passenger seat, pride swelling in his chest. "Yep. Just take it easy."

The drive to his parents' house was short, but Bo took the chance to open a conversation he'd been meaning to have.

"I've been thinking about your future," he said, watching Josh handle the car with surprising ease. Josh flicked him a quick glance.

"Yeah? What about it?"

"Well," Bo said, "it's never too early to figure out what you love doing. Something you're good at. Something that gets you up in the morning."

Josh thought about it, nodding slowly. "How do I even figure that out?"

Bo smiled, grateful his son was listening. "Just pay attention. Notice what makes you feel excited when you do it."

Josh grinned, the sunlight catching the curve of his cheek. "Okay. I'll start paying more attention."

Bo leaned back, a quiet peace settling over him.

At Lila and Henry's house, the smell of fresh cookies hit Bo the second Josh opened the car door. Henry and Jordan were chopping on freshly baked cookies as they were headed to his fathers old red pick-up truck, waving them over.

"Hey, Bo, Josh!" Henry called. "We're heading for ice cream. Josh, you coming?"

Josh was already halfway to the truck, shouting "Yeah, sure!"

Bo smiled, shaking his head. Just like that, his boy was growing up. Lila greeted him at the door, her arms wrapping around him in a tight, familiar hug.

"I'm so glad you came over," she said warmly, her voice laced with something deeper—something knowing.

Bo hugged her back, breathing in the scent of flour and vanilla that always clung to his mother's sweaters. Following her inside to the kitchen, Bo sat at the old oak table, running his hand across the worn grain as Lila set a couple of cookies in front of him.

"I heard about your dream," she said, settling across from him. "Henry told me. The elephant... and then the baby?"

Bo nodded, grabbing a glass from the cupboard for a glass of milk.

"Dad said I should ask you what you thought it meant."

Lila folded her hands, her eyes thoughtful. "I prayed about it," she said. "And I believe God showed me something."

Bo leaned in, heart thudding with a strange, raw hope.

"The baby elephant," Lila said softly, "is you, Bo. Starting a new chapter. Away from Trinity."

Bo stiffened, his stomach knotting.

"The woman leading it away," she continued, "means you need to let go. You're not meant to cling to the past. You're meant to walk forward."

Bo looked down, the cookie forgotten in his hand. *Could it really be that simple?*

"Elephants move slowly" Lila said, her voice gentle. "They're not in a rush. Maybe you shouldn't be either."

Silence fell, heavy and honest. Bo felt the truth settle deep in his gut. Lila reached across the table, her hand warm over his.

"In a couple years, Josh will be grown. You still have time to really instill some life lessons."

Bo swallowed hard, blinking against the sudden sting behind his eyes. Deflecting, he shoved his chair back with a loud scrape across the floor. He crumpled his napkin tightly in one hand, stood up, and tossed it toward the trash can. It missed, falling to the floor. He didn't bother picking it up.

Instead, he threw his head back and let out a booming laugh—too loud, too sharp, bouncing off the kitchen walls like a gunshot.

"I really messed up!" He said it between sharp bursts of laughter, like he thought if he laughed hard enough, it wouldn't hurt so much. But when he turned around—When he saw the look on his mother's face—the laughter died in his throat. Lila wasn't laughing. She wasn't even smiling.

She sat there quietly, her eyes soft and steady, looking at him the way only a mother could—straight through the bravado, straight into the bleeding place he'd been trying to hide.

And Bo crumbled. His legs gave out, and he dropped hard to his knees. The tile was cold beneath him, but he barely felt it. He pressed his face into his mother's lap, a broken sound escaping him—a sound that didn't even sound like him.

Lila wrapped her arms around him without hesitation, stroking his head as the sobs ripped free.

"Get it out, baby," she whispered, her hand moving in slow, steady circles through his hair.

So he did.

Bo wept—messy, he was gutted, uncontrollable tears—grieving not just Trinity, but every mistake, every lost moment, every piece of the life he thought he'd have.

CHAPTER THIRTY

SELENA

STRIPPED BARE

The morning sun stretched golden fingers across the ocean, casting shimmering trails over the water. Selena stood on the spacious deck of their cruise ship's presidential suite, the salty breeze teasing strands of her hair. Jordan leaned beside her, a sleepy smile on her face.

Around them, the suite radiated luxury—plush loungers, a private Jacuzzi humming quietly, and polished railings gleaming in the sunlight. Selena had spared no expense, wanting to gift Jordan something unforgettable for spring break, a memory bright enough to outshine the shadow Richard had cast over their lives.

Three months had passed since Jordan moved in with Selena's parents, a safe refuge from the chaos of an unraveling marriage. This cruise—this pocket of peace—was a much-needed escape, a breathing space to heal and gather strength.

After that final explosive fight with Richard, Selena had spent countless nights praying, thinking, planning. She put a down payment on a beautiful new home, and today—the last day of their cruise—she planned to tell Jordan.

Selena reached for Jordan's hand, her heart thudding beneath her sundress.

"Jordan, I have something important to tell you," she said, keeping her voice steady.

Jordan turned, curiosity lighting her eyes.

"What is it, Mom?"

Selena pulled out her phone and scrolled to a set of pictures. She handed it over with a tender smile.

"We're moving, sweetheart. I found us a beautiful house—near your favorite mall. It's a fresh start. A place where we can finally build the life we've always dreamed of."

Jordan's eyes widened, her excitement spilling out in a squeal.

"Really, Mom?"

Selena laughed through the lump in her throat.

"Yes, really."

She squeezed Jordan's hand, feeling the warmth of the moment settle deep inside her. Jordan flipped through the photos, her smile radiant—but then Selena caught the flicker of uncertainty in her daughter's eyes. A beat of silence passed before Jordan spoke, her voice small.

"I'm excited, Mom... but I'm really going to miss Grandma and Grandpa."

Tears welled in Jordan's eyes, and Selena's heart cracked open. She wrapped her daughter in a tight hug, rocking her gently.

"I understand, sweetie," she murmured.

"Change is hard. But we'll face it together. And Grandma and Grandpa are just a visit away."

The sun warmed their skin as they sat nestled together, their hearts soaking in the bittersweet mix of hope and loss.

The cruise had been a beautiful dream—poolside games, sun-drenched excursions, late-night talks under starlit skies. A memory chest packed full.

As the ship docked that next morning, Selena and Jordan stood side by side at the railing, watching the coastline grow closer. The once-infinite blue of the ocean gave way to the harsh concrete sprawl of the port, and with it, the bubble of peace they had floated in for days began to shrink.

Selena held Jordan's hand tightly, reluctant to let go of the rare, perfect calm they'd shared. They moved slowly through the disembarkation line, each step back heavier than the last. Selena whispered, more to herself than anyone, *"I am more than a conqueror through Christ... we will be okay, God is with us."*

By the time they stepped off the cruiseship onto California soil, the carefree smiles they'd worn onboard had faded into a shared, sober understanding.

In the car, Selena gently reminded Jordan of their plan: pack up their clothes and shoes today; the movers would handle the rest tomorrow. By morning, they would have the keys to their new life. Richard was away on business—by careful design so their paths wouldn't cross.

As they pulled into the driveway, Selena inhaled deeply, trying to steady her pounding heart. She pressed the garage remote, and the door creaked open. She leaned forward, peering into the dimness and froze.

The garage gaped empty. For a moment, her mind refused to process what she was seeing.

Where were the bikes?

The shelves of holiday decorations?

The chaotic, familiar clutter?

Instead, the concrete floor stretched out, cold and barren, echoing under the car's tires as they rolled hesitantly inside. A knot twisted hard in Selena's gut. She glanced at Jordan staring back at her, eyes wide, lips parted, but silent.

Neither of them spoke.

Selena shifted into park with trembling fingers. The usual musty smell of oil, wood, and cardboard was gone, replaced by a cold, sterile emptiness.

Everything about it felt off. Way off.

She forced herself to move.

"Come on, sweetie," she whispered hoarsely.

Jordan unbuckled wordlessly. The soft click of their seatbelts echoed harshly in the emptied garage. They stepped out into the chilling stillness, their footsteps unnaturally loud against the concrete. Selena's keys jangled in her shaking hand as she fumbled to find the house key. Jordan clutched her seashell souvenir against her chest, her knuckles white.

Selena slid the key into the lock with stiff fingers. The metal caught and gave way with a sharp click—a sound far too loud in the silence.

She twisted the knob.

And together, they stepped into an empty house.

Selena blinked, struggling to comprehend the hollow shell stretching before her. The comfortable chaos of their life—gone. Erased. A sharp knot tightened at the pit of her stomach. Their footsteps clicked unnaturally loud against the stripped floors. Echoes chased them down the empty hallways, each one a ghost of the life they once knew.

In the living room, sunlight poured through bare windows, throwing harsh light on scuff marks where family photos once hung. Only one thing remained—a single framed picture of the Bible Beatitudes, crooked on the wall, swaying slightly in the draft from the open door.

She reached out with trembling fingers, brushing the frame as her blurred eyes zeroed in on the verse:

Blessed are those who mourn, for they shall be comforted.

Tears spilled down her cheeks before she could stop them. Behind her, Jordan whimpered softly, the sound splintering Selena's heart. A chill crept over her skin as she staggered deeper into the house, flinging open doors, searching—but finding nothing.

Each hollow space struck like another blow to her chest. Jordan clung to her side, her wide, frightened eyes never leaving her mother. Selena fumbled for her phone, her fingers trembling so badly she nearly dropped it. She stabbed at Richard's number again and again.

No answer. Only a mocking, endless ring.

Then suddenly, her phone buzzed in her hand. A text. She stared at the screen, the letters sharp and cruel against the soft blur of her tears.

It read: Checkmate.

Selena reeled. *Of course. The Ring system.* He must have gotten an alert the second they pulled into the garage.

He was watching. Waiting.

Her knees buckled. She collapsed onto the cold floor as betrayal crashed over her like a wave, tears pouring as Jordan knelt beside her. Selena's scream ripped through the hollow house, raw and jagged.

"I hate him! How is this fair?" she sobbed, slamming her palm against the floor.

"Isn't evil supposed to reap what it sows?" she seethed, voice raw.

Her fury ricocheted off the bare walls. Jordan watched her, wide-eyed but silent, her small hand slipping into Selena's for strength.

"I kept having dreams," Selena whispered hoarsely.

"Dreams about Richard... and the money. When I told your grandma, she said they were warnings. She begged me to protect myself. So I pulled out every penny from our joint accounts before we left."

Jordan listened, her fists clenching. Selena wiped her face, gratitude stirring beneath the raw hurt. At least she still had something to rebuild with.

"We'll figure it out, Mom," Jordan said fiercely, her voice steady despite the fear. "We'll be okay."

Selena let the words settle in her chest like a balm. They stayed there for a long moment, collapsed on the cold, bare floor, the vast white walls and vaulted ceiling stretching high above them like a hollowed-out cathedral.

Selena felt impossibly small, a speck swallowed by the emptiness. Jordan, her brave little girl, wrapped her arms around her mother, pulling her close. Together, they clung to each other, two fragile souls stitched together by love and sheer will.

With trembling hands, Jordan bowed her head. Her voice, soft but certain, rose into the stillness, breaking it with something stronger than grief: prayer.

Selena closed her eyes and leaned into her daughter's faith. They bowed their heads together in the empty house, their whispered prayer rising like incense, stitching hope into the hush around them.

No matter what came next, they would face it as they always had—together.

Chapter Thirty-One

Lisa

Unpacking Hope

A knot of worry twisted in Lisa's stomach as she gripped her phone and connected the call with her sister-in-law, Paula. She shifted on the bar stool in her kitchen, adjusting it nervously, waiting for Paula's face to appear on the screen.

"Hey, Paula,"

Lisa greeted the moment the call connected, her voice laced with concern.

"Lisa!"

Paula's voice came through, tight with tension.

"You heard about Selena?"

Lisa took a deep breath, trying to steady her nerves.

"Can you believe Selena came back from that cruise with Jordan to find Richard emptied the house?"

They talked about the twisted irony of Richard clearing the house at the very moment Selena had already secured a new place. Paula shook her head, her disgust mirrored in Lisa's own heart.

"I wish I was there, helping unpack... think she'd answer if we tried to FaceTime her?" Lisa said firmly, her tone hardening with resolve. "I don't care how close we're not — she's my sister."

Paula hesitated, uncertain.

"I don't know. She might not feel like talking."

But Lisa's stubbornness surfaced.

"Let's try. What's the worst that could happen?"

After a little more convincing, Paula agreed. They dialed Selena's number, holding their breath as the phone rang. Lisa's heart pounded. *Would Selena answer — or shut them out?*

Lisa leaned closer to her phone as the call finally connected, the screen flashing to life.

There, in the soft light of her living room, was Selena. For a moment, Selena just stared at them — her hand hovering near the screen like she was about to hang up.Lisa's heart jumped into her throat. Paula rushed in quickly, her voice urgent.

"Hi Selena, please don't hang up."

Lisa didn't even think — her voice cracked as she blurted out, "I love you."

And then, without warning, Lisa broke. A choked sob escaped her lips before she could stop it. Hot tears spilled down as all the worry, regret, and love she'd been carrying came crashing out.

On the screen, Selena's eyes widened, startled. Even Paula froze for a second, caught off guard by the rawness of the moment. Lisa covered her mouth with her hand, trying and failing to hold it in.

"I'm sorry," she gasped through the tears. "I just... I love you. And I'm so sorry you're going through this."

The air between them shifted — thick with something deeper than words. Selena's expression softened instantly. The guarded walls that had been holding her together cracked wide open at the sight of her little sister — fiery, stubborn Lisa — falling apart for her.

A lump rose in Lisa's throat as she watched Selena slowly sink onto the couch, lowering herself like the weight of everything was finally too much to carry standing up. For a long moment, none of them said anything.

The silence wrapped around them — heavy, but healing. Finally, Selena spoke, her voice soft and uneven.

"I'm okay... Honestly... we're going to be okay. Thank God I already had a new place lined up. Financially, we're covered. Thank you both for calling," Selena said, her voice thick with emotion.

"It means more than you know."

Lisa wiped at her wet cheeks, offering a shaky smile.

"We'll always be here for you," Paula added quickly, her eyes shining.

Lisa nodded hard, swallowing against the knot in her throat.

"That's right," she said.

And then, half-laughing, half-pleading, she added, "Why can't we come over there and help?"

On the screen, Selena gave a small, real smile — the kind Lisa hadn't seen in a long, long time. And then — shockingly — Selena said, "You know what? I could use more help."

Lisa gasped. She practically launched herself off the barstool, knocking it backward as she scrambled for her purse.

"Text us the address!" she cried, already halfway to the door. Paula laughed, swiping at her tears.

"Yeah, we're on our way!"

Lisa could barely shove her keys into her hand fast enough. She shot out the door into her car, heart pounding, the urgency bubbling up in her chest. Her hands gripped the steering wheel tightly as she rushed out of her neighborhood.

Come on, come on, she willed the car, pressing harder on the gas pedal. She imagined Paula feeling the same, weaving through traffic somewhere nearby. They were both racing toward the same thing — Selena. Family.

As Lisa finally neared the neighborhood, some of the tension in her body started to ease. Her gaze swept the quiet, tree-lined streets, taking in the manicured lawns, elegant houses, and towering oaks casting cool, dappled shadows across the pavement.

Wow, she thought, slowing as she spotted Selena's new house. *She really found a beautiful place.* Lisa pulled into the driveway just as Paula rolled in behind her. They exchanged a quick glance — part surprise, part pride. Selena had landed somewhere good.

Grabbing her purse, Lisa hurried with Paula to the front door. Selena stood there waiting, her expression flickered — part relief, part vulnerability — and when her gaze landed on them, Lisa swore she saw her sister's whole body sag slightly with gratitude. Lisa didn't hesitate. She crossed the threshold and wrapped Selena into a fierce hug, Paula right behind her.

"I love you so much," Lisa murmured, her throat thick.

"We're here for you," Paula added, her voice cracking gently.

"Always," Lisa whispered.

She felt Selena's arms tighten around them as she gave in to the moment, letting them hold her up. As Lisa, Paula, and Selena exchanged hugs, the moment was suddenly interrupted.

Bo and Sam came rushing up the walkway, their faces etched with alarm. In their haste, Lisa could see them tense — mistaking them for an unexpected and unwelcome guest.

"Whoa, you guys almost got body slammed!"

Bo exclaimed, his voice tight, half-joking, half-dead serious. Sam, his brow furrowed, scanned the porch before exhaling sharply.

"I'm glad it's you guys," he said, visibly calming.

Lisa and Paula exchanged a quick glance and rushed to reassure them.

"It's just us," Lisa said quickly, holding up her hands. "We're here for Selena."

Bo and Sam exchanged sheepish glances, their bodies visibly relaxing as the tension drained away.

"Sorry about that," Bo said, scratching the back of his head. "We thought you might be someone else."

Sam chuckled under his breath.

"Yeah. Glad it's family."

Lisa laughed, the sound light and genuine, and soon everyone joined in — a shared ripple of relief rolling through them, washing away the leftover fear.

Inside, they quickly got to work, moving like a well-oiled machine. When life fell apart, family stepped in without hesitation.

Lisa, ever the detail-oriented one, immediately claimed a stack of boxes and set to sorting through them, organizing items by room. She lost herself in the rhythm — unpack, fold, stack, place — letting her hands create order from chaos. Bo, Sam, and Angel tackled the furniture, moving heavy pieces into place under Selena's quiet direction.

Lisa caught glimpses of them through the open doorways, wiping sweat from their brows, sharing quick jokes to keep the mood light. Nearby, Paula worked with Jordan and Josh, helping set up Jordan's new room. Lisa could hear bursts of laughter float down the hallway, Jordan's voice lighter than Lisa had heard in months.

The whole house buzzed with movement — the scuff of sneakers against hardwood, the rip of packing tape, the clink of dishes finding their new homes. It was the sound of rebuilding. Of life pushing forward.

As the afternoon sun dipped lower, a knock at the door sent a ripple of tension through the house again. Lisa's body stiffened instinctively.

Was it Richard? Had he found them?

Selena hesitated too, her hand hovering above the doorknob. Bo and Sam stood right behind her, silent, ready. Lisa held her breath as the door swung open — and a familiar, comforting sight met them.

It was their parents, standing on the porch, arms full of pizza boxes, wings, and Henry's famous chocolate cake.

Henry winked broadly, lifting the cake like a golden trophy. Jordan, Angel, and Josh whooped from the hallway, their faces lighting up at the sight of their grandparents. Laughter erupted, rolling through the house like a balm.

Lisa helped clear a space on the dining table as everyone crowded in, plates clattering and soda cans hissing open. Laughter mingled with the smell of pizza and chocolate, wrapping the room in warmth. Across the table, Lisa caught a glimpse of Selena — shoulders lowered, eyes glassy with unshed tears.

She didn't have to say a word. Lisa saw it. Felt it.

In the middle of all the noise, the food, and the love, her sister was finally breathing again. Not because everything was fixed. But because family had shown up.

CHAPTER THIRTY-TWO

ANGELA

WHAT'S DONE IN THE DARK

As Angela stood before the mirror in her dimly lit bedroom, she found herself able to meet her own gaze without flinching. Gone was the guilt that had once haunted her, replaced now by a fierce determination and a hunger for what lay ahead. With each stroke of mascara and sweep of eyeshadow, she reveled in the transformation taking place before her eyes. No longer did she shy away from her reflection, but instead, she embraced it with a newfound sense of confidence.

As she slipped into the seductive black dress, she admired herself in the mirror, marveling at the woman she had become. The lingering doubts and insecurities that had plagued her before were now nothing more than distant memories. Tonight, she would not hide from her desires but rather embrace them fully, unapologetically reveling in the thrill of forbidden love.

As Angela admired herself in the mirror, a brief flashback played in her mind, taking her back to the last time her mother had visited her new apartment.

When her mother had pulled her aside later, questioning if there was something going on between them, Angela had quickly spun a lie, the words slipping effortlessly from her lips. She had concocted a story about helping Dr. Darren plan a surprise party for his wife, emphasizing how uncomfortable he must have felt thinking that Angela had revealed the secret to her mother.

Angela had played the part to perfection, her expression carefully composed to convey shock and disbelief at her mother's suspicions. She had painted herself as the dutiful and trustworthy assistant, eager to maintain the façade of innocence. And as her mother had nodded in acceptance, seemingly satisfied with Angela's explanation, Angela had worn a satisfied smile on her face, knowing that her manipulation had been successful. She had shielded her secret affair from prying eyes.

Angela couldn't believe how far things had gone between her and Darren. They were seeing each other two or three times a week, fully immersed in their affair. Darren had even started giving her money and lavishing her with expensive gifts she could never afford on her own.

Despite the allure of luxury and excitement, Angela still had a nagging feeling of wrongdoing that lingered in the depths of her conscience. But just as quickly as the guilt would come, Angela pushed it aside, choosing instead to focus on the excitement.

Tonight, Darren had given her the money to hire a professional chef to prepare a meal, with instructions to ensure that the chef was gone before he arrived—a subtle reminder of the secrecy that shrouded their relationship. With a deep breath, she banished the doubts from her mind, turned away from the mirror, and headed toward the kitchen. As she stepped in, her heart skipped as she took in the scene before her.

The table was adorned with flickering candles, casting a warm glow over the room. The air was filled with the tantalizing aroma of the meal that the chef had just finished preparing—a masterpiece of culinary artistry that promised to delight the senses. A satisfied smile played on Angela's lips as she neared the table, her eye lingering on the sparkling crystal and gleaming silverware. Each place setting was meticulously arranged, the fine china adding to the atmosphere of intimacy and romance.

"Lucky guy," the chef remarked, his voice tinged with admiration. Angela returned his smile, nodding in agreement. "Thank you," she replied, reaching for her purse to pay him for his services.

With a final nod of appreciation, the chef collected his payment and made his exit, leaving Angela alone with her thoughts and the sumptuous meal that awaited her. She picked up her phone and dialed Darren's number, excitement bubbling as she informed him that everything was ready.

"Hey, babe, just wanted to let you know that dinner is all set," she said, her voice filled with anticipation. To her slight annoyance, Darren responded by double-checking if the chef had indeed left before he arrived. "Is the chef gone? I don't want any unexpected surprises," he reminded her, his tone tinged with caution. Angela sighed inwardly, feeling a twinge of irritation at his insistence.

"Yes, Darren, the chef is gone," she replied, her voice betraying her annoyance. "And don't worry, I know you're a well-respected doctor in the city. I've got everything under control."

Angela hung up the phone, irked, as she headed back to her room. As she reached for the perfume bottle, her hand hesitated over the nozzle, a wave of conflicting emotions washing over her. With each squirt of the perfume, she was layering her skin with more than just its intoxicating scent. It was as if she were coating herself in a veil of lust, deception, and deceit—each spray a reminder of the sins she was committing.

Her home, which should be a sanctuary of comfort and security, was now an open playground for the devil's devices, tempting her to stray further from everything she knew was right. She had been beguiled and given herself over to the lust of her flesh, unable to resist the thrill of the affair.

The sound of the door alert, as Darren let himself in with his key, echoed through the quiet apartment, startling Angela. She emerged from her room to meet him in the living room, her heart fluttering with anticipation. The scent of Darren's expensive cologne filled the air, enveloping her in its familiar embrace. He arrived bearing a beautiful bouquet of flowers and a small gift box from Tiffany's—a gesture that made Angela's eyes sparkle with delight.

Angela wrapped her arms around Darren's neck, the spell of lust consuming the air around them. Words were unnecessary as they lost themselves in each other's embrace, their sin igniting like a flame in the midst of darkness.

Darren's eyes gleamed with affection as he gently lifted the heart-shaped necklace from the Tiffany box and delicately placed it around Angela's neck. As the diamonds shimmered against her skin, Angela smiled and leaned into Darren's touch, the weight of the yoke he crafted settling against her collarbone. She whispered her gratitude, her voice filled with emotion as she admired the exquisite gift.

Hand in hand, they walked over to the candlelit table, the soft glow of the candles dancing in their eyes. Darren pulled out Angela's chair, ensuring she was comfortably seated before taking his place beside her. As they savored the delectable dishes and shared light conversation, the enchanting atmosphere of their dinner was abruptly shattered by the jarring ring of Darren's phone.

With a swift motion, Darren answered the call, his index finger pressed to his lips in a hasty signal for Angela to remain quiet. However, Angela couldn't help being annoyed at his gesture as he quickly excused himself from the table and disappeared through the door to take the call. Sitting there alone at the candlelit table, Angela's mind raced with the frustrations of seeing a married man.

Their rendezvous never extended beyond the confines of her house, lacking the normalcy of traditional dates. The frequent phone calls, which always necessitated him stepping away, and his strict rule that she not call after 8 p.m., were really starting to get to her. With a heavy sigh, Angela knew she had no choice but to navigate the murky waters, even at the cost of her own peace of mind.

As Darren returned to the room, Angela couldn't contain her frustrations any longer. With a mixture of irritation and longing, she voiced her desire to break free from the confines of their relationship and experience life beyond the walls of her apartment.

However, Darren's response gently reminded Angela of his prominent position as a well-known doctor, highlighting the potential scandal and repercussions if their affair were ever exposed. He emphasized their familial ties—being not only a close family friend but also her uncle Bo's best friend. Feeling the weight of his words, Angela's resolve wavered. But before she could respond,

Darren quickly turned the tables, revealing the emotional turmoil he faced in loving his best friend's niece. Angela's heart stopped.

"Did he just say he loved me?"

The fire he ignited in her burned away any doubt, drawing her irresistibly across the room to him. Their lips didn't just meet—they crashed—a desperate, knowing kiss that tasted of the addictive lie she now craved.

The words rushed from her, raw and breathless. *"I love you too,"* she whispered in his ear. It was a complete surrender to his carefully devised manipulation. The thrill of sin became like a powerful drug, clouding everything she knew was right.

And so the cycle deepened. Whenever a hint of doubt tried to break through, the strong mix of raw lust and the sweet, dangerous charm of his professed *"love"* would cast its deceitful spell. It would pull her back into the exciting, dangerous hold of his arms—her judgment and sound mind lost in the devil's plan to rob her destiny.

Being seen together in public was impossible, but to soothe her complaints, Darren masterfully planned their secret world, soon offering a new, irresistible temptation: weekend escapes.

"A secluded place," he'd murmured, his voice like a soft touch, behind his eyes a man who knew he had her right where he wanted her—keeping her mind and heart so bombarded with thrill she couldn't think straight.

He would arrange every detail, his quiet control sending a dark, exciting feeling that always kept her on the hook. The wait for his calls, the hidden getaways where those rare, stolen moments of holding hands in public became its own sweet potion that always led to the silent shadows of the bedroom. There, wrapped in the tempting light of candles, Darren created the illusion of closeness—the beautiful, deceptive fantasy of his love.

Sin enveloped her like a comforting blanket she eagerly welcomed. Angela wasn't just playing with fire—she was being changed by it.

CHAPTER THIRTY-THREE
LILA & HENRY
FAMILY MATTERS

As the morning sunlight filtered gently through the lace curtains of the cozy dining room, Lila stood at the wall with a feather duster in hand, her attention focused on a framed photograph of her beloved grandchild, Jordan.

"Missing our girl?" Henry interrupted, his attention momentarily diverted from the scattered puzzle pieces strewn across the polished surface of the table. The vibrant puzzle depicted a tranquil tropical beach, complete with crystalline waters and swaying palm trees.

"You know she'd be right here helping you," Lila remarked, shaking her head fondly at Henry's dedication to the puzzle.

"Indeed," Henry responded.

Weeks had passed since Jordan and Selena moved into their new home. A silent prayer of thanks escaped her lips, grateful for the generosity of all her children who helped Selena get settled. It was truly heartwarming to see how Sam, Lisa, and Bo had all chipped in to help Selena finish the house.

"You know, Richard still hasn't contacted them," Lila recanted, a tinge of disappointment in her voice. "He did all that showing up at Jordan's school, acting like he was truly making time for her, and now he can't even answer the phone."

Henry paused his puzzling, a shadow passing over his features as he absorbed Lila's words.

"I can't understand it," he mused, shaking his head. "After all the promises he made when he took my daughter's hand... It's just not right."

As they exchanged troubled glances, Henry's frustration with the puzzle seemed to grow.

"Ah, this puzzle is driving me crazy," Henry grumbled, his brow furrowing deeper with each failed attempt to connect pieces. "I swear, Lila, you must be hiding some of the pieces."

Lila chuckled softly, shaking her head in amusement.

"Oh, Henry, you know I would never do such a thing," she replied, her tone teasing. "Perhaps you just need to look at it from a different angle."

As Lila and Henry engaged in their playful banter, the ringing of the phone interrupted the tranquility of the moment. Lila picked up the receiver, her expression shifting to one of concern as she listened to Sam's voice on the other end of the line.

"Paula's scheduling another trip by herself," Lila repeated. She listened attentively, the tone in her son's voice tight but trying not to sound like it. It was the same one Henry had used years ago, when work almost pulled them apart. Love needed space, yes, but too much space could become silence.

"As long as the communication is open and honest, you two will be fine," she offered, her voice filled with understanding and wisdom.

Lila hung up the phone, a thoughtful frown creasing her brow as she shared the information with Henry.

"Sam needs to keep an eye on that," he remarked, his tone serious. "Redefining yourself in a marriage after the kids are gone is one thing, but too much time apart could be detrimental."

Lila nodded in agreement, but she also voiced her concern about Sam pushing back too soon.

"It's too soon for Sam to push back," she admitted, her voice tinged with a little worry. She feared that any resistance from Sam could spark deep resentment in Paula, who had supported him throughout his career.

"You know, Angel's car wash is ahead of schedule, and he'll be opening sooner than he thought. I just talked to him last night, and he told me he's planning the grand opening," Henry informed Lila with a hint of pride in his voice.

"Oh, that's awesome," Lila remarked, her eyes lighting up with affection for their grandson's entrepreneurial spirit. "Is he still going to hire Jordan and Josh?"

Henry nodded in confirmation.

"We haven't heard a peep from Angela," Henry remarked, a note of concern creeping into his voice.

Lila's fingers paused on the mixing spoon, her eyes narrowing just slightly. That look Angela gave Darren still lingered in her mind like a stubborn wrinkle in time — too soft, too familiar. It wasn't right.

"Only God knows what she could be up to," Lila remarked, her tone tinged with a hint of suspicion as she recounted the strange body language she had observed between Angela and Darren at last year's Christmas party.

"I noticed the way Angela looked at Darren," Lila sighed softly, her gaze distant as she recalled the lingering touches she had observed. "And those silly little giggles," she added, her tone troubled.

"They were dancing on the edge of something more," Henry added.

Having been married for over 50 years, age had taught them the importance of managing attractions to others. Establishing boundaries and bringing your flesh under subjection was key.

Deciding to distract themselves from their concerns, Lila asked Henry to take a break and help her bake some cookies. As Lila took out the ingredients, Henry preheated the oven.

"How did your talk with Bo go?" Henry inquired.

Lila recounted to Henry how she had been able to help Bo see that he needed to let go of the past and accept his divorce. She emphasized the importance of focusing on his relationship with their grandson Josh and being a good co-parent.

"I wonder if they'll ever get back together," Henry mused, his voice tinged with uncertainty.

"No," Lila replied firmly. "I don't think they will." She paused, gathering her thoughts before continuing.

"And you know," she added, "Bo doesn't even realize how much lighter his presence is now that they're not together."

As they moved on and discussed Josh's newfound talent for tennis, Lila and Henry began to work on making the chocolate chip cookies. Henry measured out the flour while Lila cracked the eggs into a mixing bowl.

"Well, that Josh seems to be a natural at tennis," Lila remarked, her tone proud as she folded the eggs into the mixture.

Henry nodded, a smile playing on his lips as he added the sugar to the bowl.

"He and Bo have been out at the park playing, and a coach came over saying he had a good arm and would love to coach him."

"That's great news," Lila replied, her hands busy mixing the ingredients together. "But Bo should make sure the man isn't a con."

Lila chuckled softly, her gaze shifting as she handed the chocolate chips to Henry.

"You're always so suspicious," Henry teased, sprinkling the chips into the bowl.

"My suspicions ensured that Richard didn't take all of Selena's money," she reminded him, her voice carrying a note of seriousness.

"You're right about that," Henry agreed, his laughter fading as he carefully shaped the cookie dough onto the baking sheet.

"That baby girl of yours has been real chipper lately," Lila remarked, placing the cookies in the oven and setting the timer.

"Hmm, I wonder if Lisa is seeing somebody," Henry mused, his eyebrows raising in curiosity as he leaned against the kitchen counter.

Lila nodded thoughtfully, her mind drifting to Lisa and her recent demeanor. "It's been three years since her divorce," she reflected. "It would be nice for her to start dating again."

As the doorbell rang, Henry excused himself from the kitchen to answer it. He returned moments later with Jordan by his side, a bright smile on her face.

Lila pressed a hand gently to her chest, her eyes misting as Jordan stepped into the room. The ache she hadn't spoken aloud — the one that missed her granddaughter's daily presence — softened instantly.

"Jordan, darling, it's so good to see you!" she exclaimed, her arms wrapping around her granddaughter.

Jordan explained that she asked Selena to drop her off while she went to her hair appointment. She expressed how much she missed her grandparents and how happy she was that they still kept their front door locked — a rule Jordan had implemented when she lived with them.

"Grandpa, I remembered your cliff note about dropping in on people and the gift of your time being the best gifts."

Lila smiled warmly as she watched Henry pull Jordan into a hug, feeling grateful for her understanding and appreciation.

Suddenly, Jordan's nose twitched as the aroma of freshly baked cookies wafted through the air.

"Is that cookies?" she exclaimed, her eyes sparkling with excitement.

Before they fully settled into enjoying their time together, Lila turned to Jordan with a smile.

"Jordan, sweetheart, would you mind helping me text the family about Easter dinner coming up?"

With the message sent in the family group chat, just as Henry placed the cookies on the counter and reached for one, laughter erupted as Jordan swooped in and snatched it first.

Chapter Thirty-Four

ANGEL

Grand Opening Jitters

Excitement buzzed in the air as Angel, along with his cousins Jordan and Josh, prepared for the grand opening of the car wash. It was an important day not just for Angel, but also for Jordan and Josh, as this marked their first job experience.

Despite the lack of customers at the moment, Angel remained optimistic. He knew that once the doors opened, the cars would start coming, and the real excitement would begin. He meticulously checked the state-of-the-art equipment, ensuring each nozzle was primed and ready to deliver a thorough clean.

Outside, Jordan and Josh buzzed with activity, hanging up freshly printed banners and folding drying towels.

They were practically vibrating with excitement, eager to prove themselves on their first day.

Amidst the final preparations, Angel called a meeting with his six employees, including Jordan and Josh. He opened a box and began passing out the new company t-shirts designed by Josh. Each shirt bore the logo of their business, a sleek design that captured the essence of their brand. The vibrant colors and bold graphics added an extra touch of professionalism to their appearance, signaling to customers that they were in capable hands.

With a confident smile, he addressed his team, expressing his gratitude for their hard work and dedication leading up to the grand opening.

"Team, I want to thank each and every one of you for your efforts in getting us to this point," Angel began, his voice filled with sincerity.

"Today marks the beginning of an exciting journey for us all, and I have no doubt that together, we will achieve great things."

Out of the corner of his eye, Angel caught two familiar figures slipping through the back entrance. His heart skipped — it was his mom and dad, quietly watching him with smiles that made his nerves settle a little.

His mom wiped at her eye discreetly, blinking fast like she didn't want him to notice. Angel swallowed the lump rising in his throat, wishing he could freeze this moment forever.

After charging his employees to get ready for the opening, Angel made his way over to greet them.

"Mom, Dad, I'm so glad you could make it!" Angel exclaimed, embracing them both in a tight hug. "Come with me, I want to show you around."

Leading them through the bustling car wash, Angel guided his parents to his small office in the back. Inside, he proudly pointed out the neatly organized paperwork, the computer where he would manage the books, and the desk where he planned to handle administrative tasks.

"This is where the magic happens," Angel said with a grin, his eyes shining with pride as he gestured around the office.

"We're so proud of you, Angel," Paula said, her voice filled with emotion. "You've worked incredibly hard for this moment, and we couldn't be happier for you." Sam nodded in agreement, his eyes shining with pride.

"You've built something truly remarkable here, son," he said, clapping a hand on Angel's shoulder. With a grateful smile, Angel hugged his parents once again, feeling overwhelmed with gratitude for their support.

As Sam exited the office, Paula grabbed her son in a tight hug.

"Angel, I need to talk to you," she began, her voice trembling with emotion. Angel looked at her, concern etched on his face.

"What's wrong, Mom?" he asked, his brow furrowing with worry. Taking a deep breath, Paula held her son at arm's length, her eyes brimming with tears.

"I need to apologize," she said, her voice barely above a whisper. "I've been so hard on you, frowning at your numerous attempts at entrepreneurship, not realizing that you were simply trying to find your passion."

Angel's expression softened as he listened to his mother's words. He reached out and took her hand in his, offering her a reassuring squeeze.

"Mom, it's okay," he said gently.

Paula shook her head, tears streaming down her cheeks. "No, it's not okay," she insisted. "I should have supported you no matter what, and I'm sorry for not doing that."

Angel pulled his mother into another hug, holding her close as they both let their emotions flow freely.

"Mom, I forgive you," he said softly. "And I'm grateful for your honesty and your support now. It means everything to me."

With tears still glistening in her eyes, Paula hugged her son tightly as his twin Angela stepped into the office.

"Older twin Angela reporting for duty," she greeted them with a playful salute.

"Hey, Mom," Angela said with a warm smile, giving Paula a quick hug.

"I wouldn't miss it for the world," she replied, her voice filled with pride.

Angel smiled as he watched his twin and his mom interact, feeling grateful for their presence and support on this important day. With his family by his side, he knew that the grand opening of his car wash was bound to be a success.

As the cars lined up, Angel and Angela approached Jordan and Josh, informing them that the cars were ready and it was time to open. Sensing the gravity of the moment, Angel suggested they take a moment to pray.

"Dear Lord," Angel began, his voice steady and sincere, "As we embark on this grand opening and welcome our first customers, we ask for your guidance and blessings.

May we provide excellent service and create a positive experience. We also pray for a special blessing for all who come through our doors, that you keep and protect their families."

With a shared amen, they released each other's hands and turned to face the waiting cars. And lo and behold, the first car to arrive was Uncle Bo's, accompanied by his best friend, Dr. Darren.

As Angel and Angela greeted Uncle Bo and Dr. Darren, he caught Angela shifting beside him, her demeanor suddenly stiff. Her gaze flicked briefly toward Dr. Darren — before she quickly excused herself with a nod, disappearing. He called after her, but she ignored him.

He shook off the odd moment, turning his attention back to Uncle Bo, just as more family members arrived behind them — first Aunt Selena, then Grandma Lila and Grandpa Henry. Each new face filled Angel with a surge of joy and gratitude, washing away the brief tension.

Suddenly, Josh rushed over to get Angel and told him there was a surprise waiting for him in the office.

Curious, Angel rushed right over. As he stepped inside, he was met with the unexpected sight of his Aunt Lisa, accompanied by NBA basketball player Liam Grayson.

Angel's jaw dropped in shock at the sight of the famous athlete standing before him. Aunt Lisa explained how she had convinced her friend to come and support Angel's grand opening, and Liam graciously agreed to stay for an hour to lend his star power to the event.

Angel couldn't contain his gratitude as Aunt Lisa revealed her carefully planned PR strategy to maximize the impact of Liam's presence. With a wide grin on his face, Angel swept his Aunt Lisa up into a tight hug, spinning her around in a moment of sheer happiness.

"Thank you so much, Aunt Lisa," he exclaimed, his voice filled with genuine appreciation. Turning to Liam, Angel extended his hand for a bro handshake.

"Thanks a lot, man," he said, his words sincere as he expressed his heartfelt thanks.

Without hesitation, his Aunt Lisa sprang her plan into action, calling up her nephew's social media and going live with Liam. The NBA star enthusiastically encouraged people to come and meet him at the car wash, igniting a frenzy of excitement among potential customers.

As the day unfolded, happy customers flooded the car wash, eager to catch a glimpse of Liam and experience the excitement firsthand. Liam interacted with the crowd with genuine warmth and enthusiasm, adding to the festive atmosphere of the grand opening.

As the sun dipped lower, casting a warm golden haze across the lot, Angel slipped quietly into his small office for a moment alone with God. He closed the door behind him, leaning against the desk as he exhaled deeply. Outside, the sounds of laughter, rushing water, and chattering voices rose like music.

Angel bowed his head.

"God... You see me," he whispered, his chest tight with emotion.

"You saw every night I wanted to quit. Every time I doubted myself. Thank You for holding me together when I couldn't see this day. Thank You for every hand that helped me, and for every 'no' that pushed me closer to Your 'yes.' This is Your victory as much as mine. And thank You... for letting my mom see me today. I know this is just the beginning. Keep me humble, keep me wise, and keep my heart always turned to You."

A gentle peace flooded him, steady and deep in his heart. Just as he lifted his head, a loud knock rattled the office door. Before he could answer, the door swung open — and in flooded his family and employees, faces beaming, carrying a giant cake ablaze with candles.

"Surprise!" The room burst into laughter and cheers. Angel's heart swelled as he took in the scene:

Josh and Jordan elbowing each other, his employees clapping him on the back, his parents wiping their eyes, his twin Angela grinning ear to ear. The scent of vanilla frosting filled the air.

Aunt Lisa raised her phone to capture the moment, shouting, "Make a wish, boss man!"

Angel laughed, blinking back unexpected tears as he closed his eyes for a second — not to wish for anything more, but simply to seal this moment into his memory forever. When he blew out the candles, the room erupted into applause. And deep down, Angel knew: This wasn't just the grand opening of a car wash. It was the grand opening of his new life.

CHAPTER THIRTY-FIVE

EASTER

THEY'RE ALL HERE

As Lila and Henry pulled up to the church parking lot, the anticipation of Easter service filled the air around them. Lila looked elegant in her lilac Easter dress, accompanied by a beautiful hat perched atop her head. Henry looked dashing in his tan suit, the tailored fabric fitting him impeccably and accentuating his stature. Paired with his ensemble were a pair of fancy socks, adding a touch of personality and flair. Adorning his lapel was his deacon board badge, a symbol of his years of service and commitment to the church community.

Henry had served as a deacon for years, committed to the church's spiritual and practical needs. Lila, a faithful member of the prayer warriors, was known for her fervent prayers and comforting presence. Their involvement extended beyond their roles—whether organizing fundraisers, volunteering, or simply offering a listening ear, Lila and Henry were always ready to help.

As Lila stepped into the sanctuary, she smiled warmly at her usher friend who waved them forward.

"Two rows just like you asked," she whispered, beaming with pride.

"Thank you, sweety," Lila said, setting her purse down on the row of seats. She turned to Henry, straightening the lapel on his jacket.

"They said one of the greeters called out. I told Sister Hines I'd help out in the vestibule until service starts."

Henry nodded. "Alright then. I'll take my post with the deacons." Lila gave his arm a light pat and made her way toward the lobby double doors, the scent of lilies and cologne trailing in her wake. She passed bright hats, pressed suits, and proud parents snapping photos in the aisles. At the coat rack, she slipped on a greeter sash.

Lila stood just inside the doors, greeting members with a warm smile and gentle nod. She paused when she caught sight of Sam and Paula making their way inside. Her son's hand rested lightly at Paula's back, guiding her with a tenderness that didn't escape Lila's notice.

Paula, in a soft blush-pink dress that seemed to float as she walked, looked radiant — poised, graceful, and every bit the woman Lila had once prayed her son would find. Lila smiled softly.

Just then, their steps slowed — and Lila saw they'd come face-to-face with Dr. Darren and Melissa. She couldn't hear the words, but saw the surprise on Paula's face shift into pleasant recognition.

Sam extended his hand, and Paula leaned in for a hug. Lila's smile stayed fixed, though her fingers gripped the welcome bulletin a little tighter. She stepped forward, smoothing the front of her dress as the church door swung open.

"Well look at this beautiful bunch," she said, her voice warm and affectionate. She patted Paula's arm and gave Sam a kiss on the cheek.

"Your seats are saved — second row from the front, right side."

They chuckled at Lila's slightly higher-pitched tone. The kids always teased her proper church voice. Paula gave her a quick squeeze as Lila's gaze shifted to the couple beside them.

"Dr. Darren. Melissa." She offered her hand, tone kind but measured.

"You've come quite a ways to be here, and it's always so good to see you both in God's house." Melissa greeted her graciously, and Dr. Darren gave one of his polished smiles.

"I also want to thank you both for how you've been mentoring Angela," Lila added, voice steady but lined with maternal scrutiny.

"It means a lot to our family... especially to me as her grandmother."

Dr. Darren nodded. "It's been our pleasure." Lila nodded, though something unreadable flickered behind his eyes.

The heavy oak doors of the vestibule opened again. Lila turned to see Angel and Angela coming from the opposite side. She smiled at first — her twins, always a pair — but her smile froze when Angela stepped fully into view.

A ripple passed through the crowd. Judgments formed without a word.

Angela's sexy dress — electric blue — shimmered under the chandelier. It hugged every curve. Lila blinked, her heart sinking.

Lord, not today, she thought, clutching her pearls.

The twins spotted her and walked over.

"Grandma!" Angel called out.

Angela followed, offering Lila a hug, her perfume trailing like jasmine and something too bold for Easter. Lila kissed their cheeks, her smile warm but her eyes already scanning the room.

"Your seats are saved up front," she whispered, patting Angel's arm. Then, leaning close to Angela, she added gently, "You look beautiful, baby... but next time, maybe something a little less... bold for Resurrection Sunday."

As they walked off, Angel leaned toward his sister and hissed, "I told you, you should have changed!"

Angela didn't flinch. A smirk curled across her lips — one Lila knew too well. Defiant. Sharp.

Lila's fingers shifted on her pearls as she watched onlookers gawking at Angela's dress. Angela's gaze swept the vestibule... until it landed on Darren.

Jesus. There it was. Not imagined. Not masked.

God, cover this family today, Lila prayed, hand tightening on her pearls. Her gaze caught Paula seeing Angela's dress.

No words were needed. Her daughter-in-law's expression said everything — wide eyes, lips tight, shoulders tense. Sam looked like he wanted to disappear. He glanced helplessly at Lila and rubbed the back of his neck.

"We should probably find a seat, don't you think?" Paula said, loud enough to be heard. She didn't wait, pivoting toward the sanctuary with grace just barely concealing fury.

Angel followed, shooting one last mortified glance at Angela, who — smirking — offered Dr. Darren and Melissa a polite hug. They spoke, but Lila didn't need to hear. Angela turned away with too much swing in her hips, Darren's gaze lingering too long.

Lord have mercy today, Lila muttered.

Then, the vestibule doors opened again across the lobby — and there they were. Selena and Jordan.

My babies.

Beautiful. Modest. Radiant. Selena, with her hand in Jordan's, caught Lila's eye from afar and gave a gentle nod as they walked toward her. Emotion rose in Lila's chest as she blinked back tears at the peace in her daughter's countenance. She waved them toward the sanctuary, mouthing, *"Everybody's inside — go find your seat."*

Selena answered with that soft, beautiful smile of hers, and Jordan blew her a kiss before they turned and made their way to the sanctuary doors.

Three more figures stepped into the light. Lila's breath caught.

Bo. Trinity. And Josh. Together?

Well, I'll be...

A hush moved through the vestibule. Church mothers by the coffee station squinted behind their cups.

Lila watched from across the lobby, unnoticed as they entered through the other door. Bo looked calm — maybe a little stiff. Trinity seemed lighter, a quiet kindness softening her features. And Josh, their bridge, walked between them like it was the most natural thing in the world.

Hmm okay Lord... I see you're mending.

Before she could process it, loud murmurs rose behind her. She turned from the door, where she was greeting people—and there came Lisa. On the arm of Liam Grayson. Her brows arched.

My my my, he's tall.

Heads turned. Whispers buzzed. But Lisa... she looked gorgeous. Unbothered. Confident. She wore favor — and she looked happy.

"Hi Mom, this is Liam Grayson," Lisa said, casual — too casual.

Liam smiled and reached for Lila's hand, giving it a gentle squeeze — just as stunned teens rushed over. He shook hands graciously, even as they squealed. Lila chuckled, giving Lisa a questioning look.

"I'll tell you all about it at the house, Mom," Lisa murmured, leaning in. With a deep breath, Lila nodded and motioned toward the sanctuary.

"Seats are saved," she whispered. "Two rows on the right." She watched them disappear through the doors, then straightened her hat and returned her greeter's sash to the coat rack.

Lila made her way into the sanctuary. The organist struck the opening chord. Her usher friend gave her a thumbs-up as she slipped into her seat beside Henry.

He smiled, calm and steady — reminding her why she'd loved him all these years. Lila's heart was full to have her whole family at church, yet her mind was racing from everything she'd seen.

Well Lord, they're all here. Give us a word.

CHAPTER THIRTY-SIX

THE TABLE

AND THE KNOCK AT THE DOOR

Lila sat at the head of the dining room table, her gaze drifting over the faces she loved most in the world. The scent of glazed ham, roasted vegetables, and Henry's barbecue lingered thick in the air, mingling with laughter and the faint strains of gospel music playing from the old stereo in the corner. To her, simply taking it all in was its own kind of peace. Observing was how she sharpened her spiritual lens.

From the kitchen, she heard the ladies laughing—Lisa teasing Angela, Paula beaming at Selena, Trinity's voice clear and confident. The conversation flowed like sweet tea on a hot day. It pleased Lila deeply to hear that kind of joy in her home. Not forced. Not polished. Just real.

But it hadn't all been joy.

Earlier, as she passed by the guest bedroom to refresh the hand towels, Lila had paused at the door. Inside, she could hear Paula and Angela speaking in low tones.

"Angela," Paula said, her voice edged with disappointment, "that dress you wore to church—you were in the house of God, not a nightclub."

Angela's response came sharp and without hesitation ."It's over now, Mama. You made your point."

Lila had just about turned to walk away when she heard Paula sigh.

"I just want you to carry yourself in a way that honors who you are—and whose you are."

But Angela clearly had something else on her mind.

"Uncle Bo said Darren and Melissa aren't coming to eat because he has something planned for her."

Lila's heart caught. She could see right through that child, and she prayed her crush on Dr. Darren hadn't turned into something more—especially after the looks she'd seen exchanged at church earlier that morning.

Angela's voice dipped, thick with something Lila recognized too well. Jealousy. Hurt. That bitter brew. Lila backed away quietly, the fresh towel still in her hand. She wouldn't interfere. But she would pray.

In the kitchen, she returned to Lisa and Selena embracing Trinity in warm, tight hugs.

They expressed their happiness at seeing her, assuring her that despite her divorce from Bo, she would always be family. Lila watched as Trinity's eyes glistened, her smile tight but grateful. She could see the weight lift slightly from her shoulders—the kind of relief that only comes from knowing you're still welcome.

Trinity shared how she and Bo were diligently working on co-parenting and ensuring they continued to do things together as a family for Josh's sake. Her words were met with nods of understanding and encouragement from the ladies, their hearts swelling with admiration for Trinity's commitment to putting Josh's well-being first.

Lisa's inquiry about Selena and Jordan prompted Selena to share a brief update on their adjustment. She mentioned they were settling in well and expressed her surprise at Jordan's newfound culinary skills during her three-month stay with Lila and Henry.

Selena remarked how they were enjoying their time together and the meals Jordan prepared, but she also mentioned a minor challenge they faced. She explained that Jordan sometimes acted as if Selena were her sister rather than her mother, and she had to constantly remind Jordan of their roles.

Lila didn't say much, but she took note.

Selena was doing her best, and Jordan was growing into her own—but that mother-daughter line had to be drawn. The lines had been blurred because of all that Jordan had witnessed, and she was feeling like her mother's friend.

Lila had seen it before. Children raised by strong women sometimes confused closeness with equality. It wasn't disrespect—just... immaturity. She made a mental note to pull Selena aside later, not to correct, just to encourage.

As Lila continued to observe the ladies, she realized—Selena and Lisa were actually getting along. Her eyes began to tear. This had been a long time coming.

My, my, my, Lila thought.

God works in mysterious ways.

The blow-up with Richard, had brought Selena and Lisa closer together. What once felt like a quiet tension between them was slowly turning into a genuine bond—and for Lila, that was its own kind of miracle.

As Paula joined the ladies, she came in beaming, immediately approaching Lisa with a teasing smile.

"Now, girl, I know you're a sports journalist, and Liam did you a favor by making an appearance at Angel's car wash... but church, and now here at the house? Spill the tea, honey... Are you two dating or what?"

Blushing, Lisa admitted they were. The ladies erupted in screams of joy and excitement. Lila beamed at her, saying she and Henry had a feeling she was seeing someone.

As Lila finished wrapping the foil-covered plate, she turned and gave Lisa a nod.

"Lisa, take this out to Liam. I know he's got a game, and we can't have him leaving hungry."

"I was just heading that way," Lisa said, reaching for the plate.

"I'll walk with you," Lila offered, easing down the steps with her usual grace. "I'd like to see that young man up close again," she said as they chuckled.

Across the yard near the grill, Lila spotted all the men in the family chatting it up with Liam. Angel stood a little taller than usual, his voice full of gratitude.

"I mean it, man," Angel said, reaching out for a handshake. "You being there changed everything. My followers on social media, the car wash is always busy, even the neighborhood—people are talking." Liam gave a genuine smile, gripping Angel's hand. "You've got something special, Angel. And I'd do it all again. Anything for Lisa."

Lila raised an eyebrow but said nothing. Instead, she quietly turned to Lisa and winked, then took a step back, pretending to fuss with a stray napkin caught in the breeze as Lisa approached the men.

"Thank you for today, Liam. Really," she said softly, handing him the plate.

Liam's gaze lingered, warm and easy. "I'll see you after the game." He leaned in and gave her a soft, deliberate kiss.

From the back door just behind them, a high-pitched squeal pierced the air—the ladies were watching from the doorway. Then came the whooping from the men at the grill—Henry laughing loudest of all, Sam whistling, and Angel just burying his face in his hands with a grin.

"Okay now, Lisa!"   "Ooooh, I saw that!"   "Alright, superstar—we see you!"

Lila chuckled, shaking her head as Lisa blushed and tried to wave them off.

Lila took it all in: the laughter, the love, the lightness. Henry noticed her watching and came over to plant a kiss on her cheek.

As Liam said goodbye and thanked Lila and Henry for their hospitality, they watched fondly as Lisa walked him to his car—only to be startled by two sneaky figures creeping up behind them.

"Surprise!" Jordan and Josh said in unison, holding out kiddie Easter baskets for their grandparents.

"It's your turn to get one, Grandma and Grandpa," Josh added, grinning.

Lila and Henry chuckled at the sweet gesture. She smiled down at the basket, her heart tugged by the memory of all the Easter baskets she'd lovingly filled over the years. Now that everyone was grown—including the grandchildren—she and Henry still made sure to keep the tradition alive, gifting everyone their favorite See's candy.

Lila wrapped her arms around Jordan and Josh, pulling them into a big hug.

"This is so sweet. How are my babies doing?" she asked.

They updated Lila and Henry with cheerful confidence, and like any seasoned grandmother, Lila gently sifted for more, asking after Selena and Bo. She was glad to hear they were adjusting well.

As the family gathered back inside for Easter dinner, Henry led them in prayer. And just like always, when the final "Amen" was spoken, Lila lifted her voice—and the family repeated after her:

"Oh give thanks unto the Lord, for He is good."

Lila's cheeks flushed, her eyes dancing as she looked around the table. This was the sound of family. And she knew it by heart. With appetites stirred and smiles all around, they dug into the delicious food, savoring each bite and cherishing the precious moments of joy shared in each other's company.

As the family sat around the dining table enjoying their Easter feast, a sharp knock echoed through the room from the front door adjacent to the dining area.

Jordan, ever eager, jumped up from her seat. "See, Grandma. They knocked. Didn't just walk in," she teased with a playful grin as she went to answer the door, her Uncle Bo trailing behind her.

But the moment she opened the door, her face shifted. Her eyes widened. She turned slowly—first to her mother Selena, then to the room.

A silence fell over the table.

And once again, Lila clutched her pearls—only this time, she wasn't sure whether to pray... or run.

There stood Richard.

THE END

AUTHOR'S NOTE

Before it was a novel, *The Franklins* was a stage play I wrote and produced called *Holiday Gatherings*—one of my best-selling productions. I wrote it to be lived out loud: with spotlights, applause, and a full audience leaning forward to see what would happen next.

But when the world paused in 2020, so did my productions.

And in that stillness, God whispered something new.

I started writing again—only this time, not for the stage. I found joy in going deeper, in exploring what the audience never got to see: the prayers whispered in the quiet, the thoughts characters never voiced, the wounds they carried long after the curtain call.

This book is the result of that shift.

To my longtime supporters who watched these stories unfold under the lights—this is for you. And to new readers just meeting the Franklins—welcome to the family.

If you'd like to take the journey even further, I've created a companion journal:

Reflect. Process. Grow.
Faith Through Fiction Stories
A story-inspired experience with thought-provoking prompts, reflection space, and room to explore your own story of healing and hope.

You can also stream *Holiday Gatherings* and other stage plays at:

www.nicolenewmanbooks.com

While you're there, be sure to:
- Join my mailing list for book event updates
- Follow my blog to see what I'm writing next
- Vote on which play I should turn into my next novel!

And to the dreamers—especially the ones who've had to pivot, adapt, and rediscover purpose—I hope this story reminds you:

There's still life in your gift.

Even after the lights go out on one stage, another curtain is waiting to rise.

With Love and Faith,
Nicole Newman

SNEAK PEEK

THE NEXT CHAPTER

And just before you go...

  Want a glimpse of what's coming next?

Scan the QR code below to unlock a first look at the next book in *The Franklins* series.

Let's just say... **Angela has a secret**.